THE SUMMER OF 1957
SECRETS LEFT IN THE BASEMENT

JUDITH E. POWELL

THE SUMMER OF 1957
SECRETS LEFT IN THE BASEMENT

iUniverse books may be ordered through booksellers or by contacting:

iUniverse
1663 Liberty Drive
Bloomington, IN 47403
www.iuniverse.com
844-349-9409

ISBN: 978-1-6632-1502-4 (sc)
ISBN: 978-1-6632-1501-7 (e)

Library of Congress Control Number: 2020925189

Print information available on the last page.

iUniverse rev. date: 01/29/2021

To all the young girls whose voices have never been heard.

and

To Mimi, my mother, whose dedication to keeping a daily diary inspired this book.

PROLOGUE

THE BASEMENT—DAYTON, OHIO, 1957

PENELOPE RAN BAREFOOT down the stairs to the basement, jumping to the concrete floor from the second step, her blonde ringlets bouncing with delight. The cool concrete felt good to her warm, young feet. The basement was one of her favorite places to play in the summer. It was the coolest spot in the house on a hot summer day.

All the houses on her street had basements, as did most of the homes in her town. Many of the basements had been transformed into another room, a precursor to the family den. Ground-level rectangular windows bordered the basement, letting in daylight.

Her family's basement walls were painted sky blue. A hand-me-down sofa from Penelope's grandparents sat along one wall with a floor lamp at one end. A rocking chair occupied the space to the side of the sofa with a small table and lamp. Her mother had braided and stitched together a multicolored rag rug made from fabric remnants, and two colorful pillows brightened up the brown sofa. An oblong table with four mismatched chairs was used to play games and do crafts. For their summer craft project, her mother had purchased paint-by-number kits. By mid-June Penelope had completed one picture, now proudly displayed above the sofa. Under the basement steps, Penelope's dad had enclosed a small area, providing a playhouse where she had her dolls and doll furniture. She spent many hours playing dolls with a friend or by herself.

The basement also housed the wringer washing machine and a tub for rinsing clothes and other items. In warm weather, clothes hung on lines outside to dry. In the winter, a clothesline was strung from wall to wall in the basement. An ironing board was a standard fixture there in the summer months, providing a cool place to do the weekly ironing.

The home was heated by a coal-burning furnace which occupied a portion of the basement. Near the furnace were two small rooms, each with a window and a door. One of the rooms was for coal storage. Every September, a large truck lumbered up the street with a load of coal and dumped it through the window and into the room. The other room stored food that had been canned during the summer, along with out-of-season equipment—sleds and snow shovels in the summer, bikes and garden equipment in the winter months. The house did not have a garage.

There was nothing dismal or frightening about a basement for Penelope—at least not until the summer of 1957.

------◆◆◆------

1993

Thirty-six years later, Penelope, no longer a child, is forced to go into the basement of her memories to finally reconcile what took place in a basement on a sunny summer day in 1957.

1

DENVER, COLORADO—OCTOBER 1993

THE LETTER ARRIVED addressed to Penelope Evans Parker with the return address from Elizabeth W. Scott in Dayton, Ohio. The name was not familiar to Penelope, so she assumed it was some kind of chain letter or promotional advertisement. She put it aside with other junk mail to go through when she had more time. Two days later, after slicing the letter open, she felt a business card fall into her lap as she pulled out the letter and began reading the first paragraph.

> *Dear Penelope, I don't know if you will remember me. I am Elizabeth, and we were friends when we were seven and eight. My grandparents were Mildred and Edward Werner who lived in Dayton, Ohio, on the same street where you lived. Their house was at the end of the street and your home was in the middle. I spent weekends and most of the summer with my grandparents. We were constant playmates. You were my best friend.*

Penelope sat holding the letter in her quivering hands. The pit of her stomach filled with fluttering butterflies, and she was overcome with a queasy feeling that something dreadful was about to happen. She moved from her comfortable living room chair to a chair in the kitchen, where she would be closer to a sink in case she threw up.

She knew who Elizabeth was and where her grandparents had lived. Some names and places remain forever in your memory as though they were hard-wired into your brain, guaranteed to surface when you heard them again. Thoughts raced through Penelope's mind. Why after thirty-six years was Elizabeth contacting her? How did she know her married name and where she lived? After Penelope graduated from high school, her family had moved to a suburb south of Dayton. She had gone to college, moved to Colorado, married, and was now living in Denver—thirteen hundred miles from her hometown in Ohio.

Penelope took a deep breath to calm her pounding heart. She willed herself to read on.

> You may recall, in the summer of 1957, you had a party for your eighth birthday. I have enclosed a picture taken around your dining room table with all of us in party hats eating cake and ice cream. To refresh your memory, I am the one next to you on the right.
>
> Your birthday party was the last time we were together. In the days following the party, whenever I went to your house, your mother said you were busy or not there. But then, I would see you riding your bike or walking to the ice cream truck. I was heartbroken and wondered why you didn't want to continue our friendship.

A month later, my grandparents moved to a new neighborhood on the other side of town. A few weeks after they moved, my grandfather disappeared. His body was found two days later in his car on an abandoned country road with a gunshot to his head. His death certificate stated, "Suicide from gunshot to right side of head." There was a notation on the medical examiner's notes stating, "Suicide could not be 100 percent determined."

I am sure you are wondering why, after all these years, I am writing you. To give you some background, after I graduated from high school, I obtained a degree in criminology from Ohio University. I am an investigator for the Dayton Police Department. We have been reviewing some unsolved murders. My grandfather's death has puzzled me, and although his is not one of the cases we are pursuing, I have been working on it in my spare time. I have reviewed documents from the Dayton police files concerning his death and the medical examiner's report. Those reports have made me wonder if my grandfather had been involved in something that caused him to commit suicide or to be murdered.

My memories of my grandfather are of a kind, loving man. I can't imagine why he would commit suicide or be murdered.

I would like to talk with you or meet with you the next time you are in Dayton visiting your family. I have read about you and your husband's work in seeking justice for people wrongfully accused of a crime. Since you

knew my grandparents, I am hoping you
will consider helping me to learn whether
his death was suicide or homicide and why.
I want this for my peace of mind and justice
for my grandfather if he was murdered.
  Sincerely,
    Your long-ago friend, Elizabeth Werner
Scott

Penelope stared at the letter in disbelief. She read it two more times. Then with a vengeance, she tore the birthday picture into tiny pieces and ground them in the disposal. She did not need a picture to remind her of her eighth birthday party. It was her last birthday party as a child. In the years following, her mother would suggest having a party with school friends, but Penelope only wanted a party with family.

Penelope had not blocked that summer out of her mind, but it was not something she dwelled on. Years ago, she had come to terms with the summer of 1957. Still, no amount of time can ever completely erase some memories. Some scars always remain but can be camouflaged with time. Penelope had been successful at camouflaging hers.

She considered telling her husband about the letter. Then again, she had never told David about the incident when she was eight. Elizabeth's letter would give her the opportunity to tell him. It might help him to understand her hang-ups. However, over the past year, David had seemed to be constantly annoyed with her. Earlier in the day, she had asked him to pick up batteries for their flashlights because an early ice storm was expected. She feared the electricity would go out, which it often did. It was a small request, but he had turned it into a major argument. "You need to grow up, stop acting like a child, and learn to sleep without a light on all night!" David had shouted at her, slamming the door on his way out. With his recent attitude toward her, she decided now was not the time to involve him.

After pacing around the house for a couple of hours, Penelope responded to Elizabeth's letter and dropped it in the mailbox.

> *Elizabeth, I cannot help you. The work my husband and I do through our charity is not to solve crimes. Our efforts are to help exonerate those who have been wrongly convicted. Therefore, there is no need to contact me for further information. I did not know your grandfather was dead, but perhaps he received justice. PEP*

After Penelope mailed the brief note to Elizabeth, she went through the rest of her day in motion only, trying not to think about the letter. She began to doubt her impulsive decision to respond so quickly to Elizabeth.

2

EDWARD WERNER WAS dead! He was not only dead, but dead from a gunshot to the head. Elizabeth's letter was the first Penelope had heard that Werner had died in 1957. How could she have known? She was eight years old and would not have been reading the newspaper, assuming it *was* in the paper. If her parents knew of his death, they didn't tell her. In fact, this was the first time she had heard that Mr. Werner's first name was Edward and his wife was Mildred. They had always been Mr. Werner and Mrs. Werner.

Penelope hoped she would not hear from Elizabeth again, although she suspected Elizabeth would not give up on her quest to learn more about her grandfather's death. Still, Penelope had to admit her curiosity had been piqued. She wondered about the circumstances of Werner's death since it was close to that summer day in 1957.

Over the years, Penelope had never given any, or at least not much, thought to what had happened to the Werners. The rest of that summer, Penelope had avoided going by their house. She remembered one day in late September, she'd been on her front porch teaching her dolls their ABCs when a young woman with a baby stroller walked by Penelope's house. The woman smiled and gave a wave. Penelope took it as an invitation to see her baby. Talking to the young mother, she learned the Werners had moved. The woman told her she and her family had moved into the last house on the street— the Werner house. Penelope recalled feeling relieved when she heard they had moved. Now, she would be able to ride her bike or walk to the end of the street and not be afraid of seeing him.

Nine days after the first letter, Penelope received a second one from Elizabeth. The letter was brief.

> *Penelope, thank you for replying to my letter. The last line in your response has confused me and left me with questions. We must talk. Please call me at your earliest convenience. Enclosed is my business card with my contact phone numbers. I hope to hear from you soon. Elizabeth*

Penelope knew she had opened Pandora's box and would need to find out more about Edward Werner's death before she talked to Elizabeth—if, in fact, she decided to contact her. She had a trip planned to Dayton, Ohio, during the last week of October to visit her parents and her brother, Paul, and his family. She would use the visit to find out what her parents knew about Werner's death. But first, she planned to do some research prior to leaving for Ohio.

The next week, Penelope contacted Dayton's main library to get the 1957 obituary for Edward Werner. Her call was directed to the archive department where, she was told, Reed Remington, a college journalism student, was working part-time. Reed informed her that all obituaries were on microfiche and finding Edward Werner's obituary would be easy. In less than fifteen minutes she received two faxes. A brief obituary had appeared in the Dayton morning paper, *The Journal Herald*, and in the evening paper, *The Dayton Daily News*, on Monday, September 23, 1957. It stated that Edward A. Werner had passed away on September 13, 1957, at the age of fifty-six. He was born in West Virginia. His family moved to Dayton when he was fourteen. He had been the purchasing manager for a manufacturing company as well as a member of the Dayton Rotary Club and Grace Lutheran Church. He was survived by his wife of thirty-three years, a daughter, and a granddaughter (they were not named). There were private graveside services, but no date was mentioned and no funeral home was listed.

Penelope called Reed to thank him and to ask if he would search for articles in the Dayton papers about a man found shot in his car between the dates of September 13 and September 23, 1957. Reed was eager to help. Quicker than Penelope thought possible, he called back and read her the articles.

An article on September 16, 1957, had appeared in the local news section of *The Dayton Daily News.*

> On September 15, 1957, the body of a Dayton man was found in his car on an abandoned country road off State Route 48, dead from a gunshot wound to his head. The man, dressed in a suit and tie, appeared to be going to work or coming home from work. The medical examiner stated he had been dead for approximately forty-eight hours. Police indicated it was a suicide, although no note was found at the scene. Investigators are talking to family, work associates, and friends before releasing his name.

Reed wasn't able to find any additional articles except for two sentences on September 20, 1957.

Man found dead in his car of a gunshot wound to the head on September 15, 1957, has been identified as 56-year-old Edward A. Werner of Dayton. His death has been ruled a suicide.

3

DAYTON, OHIO—OCTOBER 1993

PENELOPE ARRIVED AT the Dayton airport and was greeted by her adoring parents with smiles and hugs. She had taken the latest John Grisham book, *The Client*, to occupy her time on the flight from Denver, but she found her mind drifting to Elizabeth's letter and Edward Werner's death. How was she going to approach her parents for information on Werner's death? One thing she had to do was read her mother's diary from the summer of 1957. Her mom had begun keeping a daily diary when she was a teenager. She called it her therapy. The diaries were kept in a box in the back of the guest bedroom closet. It would be easy to find, if Penelope got the opportunity. She would make sure she got the opportunity.

Waiting to collect her luggage, her mom chattered about what she had planned for her visit, who they would see, the trendy new places to eat, and the shops to explore. Dottie Evans was a petite five-foot-two dynamo when it came to organizing events and shopping. She worked part-time at an upscale boutique in a small shopping mall, where she loved the interaction with people. It kept her up on the latest fashion trends and local gossip, which she readily shared with her daughter. For Penelope, visiting her parents was a real get-away vacation. She didn't have to worry about making plans or decisions on what they would do; her mom handled those details. But, on this trip, Penelope needed time on her own to do a little digging into Edward Werner's death. She had brought Elizabeth's business card in case she decided to contact her.

Her dad's routine when driving home from the airport was to take the scenic route instead of the freeway. Now in late October, the drive was beautiful with radiant gold, red, and orange fall colors dominating the landscape. Penelope looked forward to the forty-five-minute drive with its familiar landmarks and her mother pointing out the new developments and changes in Dayton.

When they finally pulled into the driveway of her parents' suburban home, Dottie said, "We have a surprise for you, Pen."

Penelope wasn't sure she could handle any more surprises. "Oh? What kind of a surprise?"

"We have done some rearranging of the bedrooms. My former bedroom is now back to being the guest room. We still use the closet in the room to store a few things, but I have moved most of my clothes. You will have plenty of space for your belongings."

"Wow, that sounds great! So, you two are now sleeping in the same room? Sparking up the old romance, are ya?"

Chuckling, Dottie went on, "Well, your dad's snoring has improved since he had treatment for a bad sinus infection last winter. Either that or my hearing is going. Whichever, we seem to manage fine sleeping in the same room now. We bought a king-size bed and redecorated the master suite. You'll love it. I used your favorite colors."

"Good for you. I can't wait to see it."

Her parents had started sleeping in separate bedrooms when they had both been working downtown so her mom could get a good night's rest, free from her dad's snoring. Penelope never doubted her parents' affection for one

12

another and knew there was a well-worn path between the two bedrooms.

It was after eleven o'clock when everyone finally went to bed. Penelope was tired from traveling, but she was itching to see if the box of diaries was still in the guest bedroom closet. Hanging up her clothes, she noticed the box in the far end of the closet. Easing it to the center of the closet, she looked for the 1957 diary. She found it and turned to the month of July. To her surprise, the pages from July 22 to September 16 were blank. Why were those pages blank? It didn't make sense. Her mother was a fanatical record keeper. Not keeping an accurate account of a significant family event was not at all like her—unless her mother was so distraught she couldn't write about the experience, but that didn't add up either. Putting her thoughts and experiences on paper was how her mother handled problems and coped with issues.

Disappointed, Penelope used her foot to scoot the box back into the corner of the closet.

4

PENELOPE TOSSED AND turned trying to fall asleep. Sleep finally came, but her subconscious mind was still dwelling on the blank pages. At five o'clock, she awoke with a sudden realization: her mother must have kept a separate journal for those dates in 1957. She turned on the bedside lamp and, being careful not to make a sound, pulled out the box. One by one she laid the diaries on the floor, taking special care so she could put them back in the same order. In the bottom of the box was a large brown envelope. Opening the metal clasp, she pulled out a spiral notebook and began reading.

Monday July 22, 1957—Had a sickening shock tonight. Mr. Werner from up the street is having a movie for the kids in the neighborhood tomorrow night, but Pen wouldn't go and at bedtime told me why. She is friends with his granddaughter, Elizabeth. She was at Pen's birthday party on Saturday. Elizabeth won a prize, which she forgot. Yesterday, Pen went to the Werners' house to take the prize to her, but Mrs. Werner had left to take Elizabeth back home.

Werner invited Pen to watch part of a movie he planned to show the neighborhood kids on Tuesday. He wanted her to choose from several movies and select the one kids would like best. The movies were in his basement. In between Pen's gasping sobs she finally was able to tell me the hideous details. It was all I could do to hold it together. She begged me not to tell her father as the bastard said he would kill her if she told anyone. I gave a slight nod in agreement, but I had to tell Walt. (Parents don't keep things of this magnitude from one another.)

Walt is an easygoing, mild-mannered man (to the point it sometimes irritates me), but when I told him about Pen, he was as angry as I had ever seen him. I thought he was going to go up and have it out with Werner, but assault and battery was not the way to handle it. After we both calmed down, he went to talk to Charles Taylor, a neighbor three doors down who is a detective on the police force. Taylor said they would bring Werner in for questioning.

I checked on Pen almost every hour during the night as sleep was not possible. Walt didn't get much sleep either.

Tuesday July 23, 1957—Walt received a call at his office to come down to the police station to talk about the incident. He has connections with law enforcement due to his position in charge of security at the General Motors plant and his previous years

16

on the Ohio State Patrol. The police will bring Werner in for questioning tomorrow.

I cancelled bridge tonight. Don't want to leave Pen even though Walt is home. In no mood to make light conversation and act like all is fine. I may look for another house—scared to stay here. Werner had his movie tonight for the kids. Paul was upset because we would not let him go. He didn't understand why he couldn't go just because Pen didn't want to. I told him Mr. Werner was a bad man and he is to stay away from his house. He didn't ask for any details.

Wednesday, July 24, 1957—The police had Werner in for questioning. Walt was present. Werner denied everything, but the police didn't believe him. Walt warned him to stay away from our children. If we have him arrested, Pen will have to describe her experience and possibly tell it to a court. I would dread it for her. At this point, she doesn't know I told her father or that the police are involved. What to do? Werner now knows she told. I pray he also is not a murderer. What a nightmare this is!

Werner supposedly is a respectable citizen—close to sixty. What a slimy bastard! I think I could kill him with my bare hands. Hope I never run into him. Wonder what his wife thinks or what she knows? How could anyone stay married to such a person?

Thursday, July 25, 1957—Last night when I checked on Pen, she had closed and locked her two bedroom windows. It has been a hot summer, and open windows are the only relief we get at night. I imagine she is afraid Werner will keep his promise and climb in a window while she is sleeping and kill her, even though the bedrooms are upstairs. She is insisting we leave the hall light on all night. Paul says it shines right in his bedroom, and last night he got up and turned it off. Around three a.m. Pen woke up. When she realized the light was off, she cried out for me. Both Walt and I ran to her bedroom, nearly falling on each other. We calmed her down. I slept the rest of night with her. Walt will make some kind of small night lamp to put in her room, and we will put a fan in her room.

Friday, July 26, 1957—Paul asked me if Pen was sick. He said she was acting strange. She runs in the house when she sees Elizabeth coming down the street, and she only rides her bike in front of the house. He wondered why she had to have the light on all night and why she screamed in the middle of the night. I said she was not sick but she had a bad experience and needed time to get over it.

Monday, July 29, 1957—Betty Mueller came by the house this afternoon. Pen and Paul were at Mom and Dad's. Betty lives on the other side of the street two doors down from the end. Her daughter, Joyce, and Pen play together occasionally. Joyce is ten. Betty seemed nervous coming to the door. I invited her to have some lemonade. Last night Joyce told her about an incident with Werner. Joyce had gone to the movie he had for the kids last week. Werner told her he had a lot of children's movies and she was welcome to come over and see them anytime.

Yesterday, Werner was on his front porch when Joyce was outside. He invited her to watch a movie. Joyce went down in the basement where he started to show a movie. Her account started similar to Pen's, except Joyce was able to get away before it escalated. Werner threatened her with death the same way he did Pen.

Betty knew our children had not gone to the movie and wondered if one of our children had an incident with Werner. I gave her a brief description of Pen's experience but didn't go into all the details—too painful for me and unnecessary at this point. I let her know that Walt had talked to Detective Taylor and the police took Werner in for questioning.

Betty's husband, John, is a truck driver and will not be home till tomorrow. I suggested her husband call Walt when he returns home to discuss how to handle the situation. Walt would want the police to be notified about Joyce's incident.

Betty has two younger daughters ages seven and five. She is concerned for them. She doesn't know how she can go on living across the street from the Werners. She thought they were friendly, decent people. Ed Werner had shoveled her sidewalk and helped her with a minor household problem a few times when her husband was on the road. He was polite, a perfect gentleman, and very helpful. Now she realizes he was only trying to gain the trust of her girls.

Tuesday, July 30, 1957—After dinner John Mueller called Walt. They met at the Muellers' house. Walt said, "John is a good guy, a family man with a traveling job. He is concerned about leaving his wife and three young girls when he is on the road." Naturally, he was upset to get this disturbing news and said he would like to go over and cut Werner's balls off and hang them from the lamppost in his front yard. Walt suggested they both go to the police tomorrow.

Wednesday, July 31, 1957—Walt made arrangements for them to meet with Detective Taylor today. An officer from the department who handles child sexual abuse was also present. The police plan to go to Werner's home this evening to bring him in for questioning again. Officers will interrogate him along with an expert on pedophiles.

Betty Mueller had Joyce write about her experience to give to the police. It was helpful for the police and gave them more information about how he operates. Joyce is a mature and bright ten-year-old. Being the oldest of three, she has more responsibilities at home caring for her younger sisters and with household chores.

Thursday, August 1, 1957—Walt got a call at work from Larry Mann; he is the expert on pedophiles. He spent over an hour with Werner last night. Werner continued to deny any involvement even when Joyce's written statement was put in front of him. His comment was, "That girl has quite an imagination."

After several hours, Werner refused to answer any more questions. For now, they have released him. Mr. Mann wanted to know if our daughter would be willing to give a tape recording of her experience. They would do the recording in our home with only Larry Mann present so it would not be as intimidating for her. Walt and I need to discuss this since Pen does not know the police are involved.

Mann told Walt, "Nobody can tell a lie like a pedophile. Lying becomes their way of life, to the point they begin to believe their own lies. They are monsters who want to perform a sex act with children. Pedophiles can't justify what they do, nor can we. They hide what they are from family, friends, and the world. Many are so-called pillars of society, church going, teachers and coaches—all living a lie. When pedophiles are incarcerated, they have to be separated from the general prison population. Hardened criminals can't tolerate a pedophile."

Friday, August 2, 1957—John Mueller came to our house. He wanted to go to Werner's house and confront him. Walt tried to talk him out of it, but he was insistent. Walt told him it would be better if the two of them went together, and John agreed.

John Mueller is a big man, over six-foot, with a barrel chest, big arms, and big hands. He played football in high school and had a football scholarship to the University of Tennessee. He and Betty met in his sophomore year, married, and started a family right away, or the family was started before they married. He had to quit college to get full-time work to support his wife and baby. He is in his early thirties, with a thick head of blond hair, deep blue eyes, and charming dimples when he smiles. His face is soft and youthful—a young, boyish look. It makes me think when he was being put together they placed the wrong head on his body or vice versa.

Saturday, August 3, 1957—Walt filled me in on what transpired when he and John went to Werner's house. Werner came out on the porch with a "shit-eating grin" on his face, greeting them with "Hello, fellas" as though they were there to drink a beer and talk sports. Walt said John would have coldcocked him if he had not grabbed his arm. John shouted at Werner, "We know what you've done to our daughters and to other girls! You're not going to continue getting away with molesting children. The police know about you. It's only a matter of time till they arrest you!"

Werner's comment was, "You have no proof—only the imaginations of two little girls. Those girls came to my house of their own free will. I never grabbed them off the street. You boys don't know what you are talking about.'

John grabbed Werner by the collar of his shirt and warned him to stay away from his house and his family. John told him he was scum and needed to be eliminated from the face of the earth. We both feel the same way. It would be a blessing if he'd drop dead.

Dear God, give me the strength to get through this most difficult time.

5

PENELOPE STOPPED READING. Sitting on the floor and leaning against the bed, she rubbed her forehead, trying to digest what she had read. She felt overwhelmed with all this new information and shocked by some of her mother's words. She had never heard her mother use profanity. Occasionally, her dad shouted "damn" or "hell" at something on TV, but his ire was always directed at a sporting event or a politician. Penelope sensed her parents' rage permeating the pages of the journal—her mother writing she could kill him with her bare hands and her parents and John Mueller all wishing he would die. It made Penelope wonder: how much did her parents know about Edward Werner's death? Was it possible they had something to do with it? She pushed the thought out of her mind.

The sound of the toilet flushing in her parents' bathroom nudged her back from her thoughts. She turned off the bedside lamp, hurriedly put the journal back in the envelope, and tucked it under the bed. She wanted to finish reading before daylight so the journal could be returned to its hiding place in the bottom of the diary box.

It was six o'clock, too early for either of her parents to

be up and earlier than she wanted to start the day. But going back to sleep would not be possible. Not hearing any more stirring sounds from her parents' room, she took a flashlight out of the nightstand and the envelope from under the bed and started reading again.

Monday, August 5, 1957—I saw Mildred Werner at the grocery store this afternoon. I wanted to avoid her, but when I turned in an aisle, there she was. She was pleasant, asking how we all were. I wanted to say, "Why don't you ask your child molesting husband?" but of course I didn't. She said Elizabeth was coming to their house this week and asked if she could take the girls to a movie. Fortunately, Pen is going to spend the rest of the summer with her grandparents in West Virginia.

Wednesday, August 7, 1957—Elizabeth came to the house this morning asking if Penelope wanted to ride bikes. I told her she was busy getting ready to go to her grandparents in West Virginia. I feel sorry for little Elizabeth; she and Pen were good playmates. I know she doesn't understand why Pen doesn't play with her anymore. I imagine she gets the same reaction if she goes to the Mueller house. Such a shame as she is a sweet child. Makes my blood boil when I think how many lives he has hurt.

Thursday, August 8, 9, 10, 1957—We left Thursday. Pen was thrilled to learn she was going to Grandma and Pop Evans for the rest of the summer. We spent three days in Glenville before leaving Pen. Right away there was a noticeable change in her—she was more talkative, laughing, having fun with her cousins, eating more than she has since her birthday. I am sure she has a sense of relief not having to worry about "the monster" coming after her. My heart breaks for her. Will she ever get past this? I suppose so, but when and at what price?

Sunday, August 11, 1957—We arrived home after dinner. Knowing Pen is safe and enjoying time with family allowed me a restful night of sleep.

Monday, August 12, 1957—Paul came running in the house this afternoon announcing there was a police car at the Werners' house. I casually said maybe they had a robbery. He wanted to know why Mr. Werner was a bad man. I told him Mr. Werner uses bad language around children and tries to be too friendly with young girls. He seemed to accept my explanation.

Where is the handbook on how to handle a situation like this? I have seen books on raising babies, children, preteens, and teenagers and books on helping a child deal with a death, but nothing on how to help when your child has been sexually molested.

Tuesday, August 13–August 18, 1957—The week was quiet, no crisis and nothing mentioned about the situation.

Monday, August 19, 1957—I collapsed when Walt came home from work this afternoon and told me Werner had been spotted driving around Walt's parents' home in Glenville this past weekend. Walt had informed his mom and dad about Pen's experience so they would understand if she was quieter than usual or if she insisted they leave a light on in the hall at night. On Saturday, Pop Evans was working in the yard when he noticed a man in a tan Oldsmobile drive slowly by twice, thirty minutes apart. Later he was sitting on the front porch and saw the same vehicle. He made a note of the license plate. On Sunday morning, Pen, her cousins, and her grandparents attended church. When leaving the church, Pop Evans saw the same car. This morning he called Walt at work to let him know about the car and gave him the license number. Walt knew Werner drove a tan Oldsmobile. Walt called Detective Taylor and had him run the license plate. It was Edward Werner's car.

It felt like a sledgehammer was pounding my heart. I couldn't breathe, my knees buckled, my eyes blurred, and I crumbled to the floor. Walt wanted to take me to the hospital. I refused. It would require too many questions. How did Werner know where Pen was? Then I remembered my conversation with Mildred Werner in the grocery two weeks ago. I didn't think about it at the time, but Mrs. Werner mentioned they had family in West Virginia and asked what part Walt's family was from. I told her Glenville. She had obviously mentioned it to her husband. It would be easy for Werner to find the addresses. He knew Walt was a "Junior," so all he would have to do was stop at a phone booth in Glenville and look up Walter Evans to get the address. There was only one Walter Evans in Glenville. I never considered a casual grocery store conversation in the cereal aisle would lead to this.

What was Werner's purpose in going to Glenville? Was he going to try to kidnap Pen? Murder her? Surely, he would not be that stupid. He would be the first person the police would suspect.

Two detectives picked Werner up at his place of employment today. Taylor told Walt they could not arrest him for driving around Glenville but they could lean on him hard.

No sleep tonight for either of us.

Tuesday, August 20, 1957—I am concerned about Paul's safety. Fortunately, he has been staying home working on his pirate ship in the basement. I decided to alert Marjorie, our next-door neighbor, about Werner. She has two young children. I also informed the Hadleys, who live across the street. They are a retired older couple with grown children. They spend a lot of days on their front porch in the summer. If they see anything suspicious, they will let us know.

Wednesday, August 21, 1957— Detective Taylor called Walt, telling him Werner admitted he had been in Glenville. He told the police he drove over to visit family in another town, got lost, and was driving around trying to get his bearings. He did not have a map. Werner admitted he drove up and down several streets more than once. He stayed Saturday night with family outside of Glenville in Gilmer, West Virginia, and came home Sunday afternoon. He insisted on giving the police the phone number of his family to prove he was there. When asked why his wife did not go with him, he said she had to babysit their granddaughter.

Werner asked the police how they knew he had been in Glenville. They told him his car was reported several times driving in various neighborhoods and parked near a church Sunday morning where the Evans were attending. He claimed he had no idea who went to that church. He had merely chosen a place to park to look at a map he had just picked up at a gas station. The police do not believe him, but they can't arrest a man for claiming to be lost and driving around a town.

Saturday, August 24, 1957—Betty Mueller called to tell me there was a truck at the Werner house loading boxes and furniture. They are moving. What a blessing for us but unfortunate for the neighborhood where they are moving. Seems like someone should warn them. Too bad you can't brand him with a big red "P" for *pedophile* like the "A" for *adultery* that Hester Prynne had to wear in the *Scarlet Letter*.

We are going next week to pick up Pen in Glenville and get her ready for school. Walt and I discussed whether we should tell her the Werners have moved. We decided not to as she has been doing so well and it might bring up bad memories.

Penelope flipped the page over, but the next page was blank. There were no more entries in the journal, but it was obvious pages had been torn out of the spiral notebook.

Penelope dropped the notebook in her lap, her mouth hanging open slack-jawed. Why did she have to learn this by sneaking to read her mother's private journal? She understood why her parents hadn't told her about the police involvement, but they should have let her know the Werners had moved and, later, that he had died. The idea they thought it "might bring up bad memories" annoyed her. Did they not realize those "bad memories" would be with her the rest of her life?

Reading the journal armed her with crucial information. She would need to give more thought on how to bring up the subject with her parents without revealing any of the details she had read in the journal. Again, the fearful thought entered her mind: What did her parents know about Edward Werner's death? It was inconceivable to think they had any involvement in a murder scheme—or was it?

6

SHORTLY AFTER SEVEN o'clock, Penelope grabbed her robe and headed to the kitchen for a strong cup of coffee. While her parents still slept, she took the warm mug of coffee to the den. She sat on the sofa with her legs curled under her, staring at her reflection in the glass screen on the fireplace. Why did this have to resurface now? She contemplated forgetting about bringing up the subject with her parents and just let sleeping dogs lie. However, judging from the tone in Elizabeth's letter, she sounded determined to find out about her grandfather's death. Penelope needed to talk to Elizabeth before she got her parents involved. She would tell Elizabeth about her grandfather, and maybe that would be the end of it. Now that Penelope knew the police had been involved and were about to arrest Werner, it seemed reasonable to believe he would commit suicide to avoid going to prison.

Daylight began to peek through the windows when Penelope was jarred from her thoughts by the ringing of her parents' phone. Her dad emerged from the bedroom, tying his robe saying, "Your mom had a call from Cynthia at the store. I hope it didn't wake you."

"No, Dad, I've been up. I made the coffee."

"Thanks. Making the coffee is usually my job. There is a coffee cake on the kitchen counter. I know you like something sweet with your coffee. Why are you up so early? Did you not sleep well?"

"The time change affects my sleep for the first night, but I got enough rest."

"Your mom and I don't rush into our days anymore unless we have an early appointment. We enjoy our coffee, read the paper, and discuss our plans for the day. Two or three days a week she works at the store—er, uh, the *boutique*, as she calls it—but she doesn't need to be there till ten. If I'm playing golf, I leave before she does."

"Sounds like you have it all worked out."

"Yes, we do. There was a time when we weren't on the same page or, for that matter, even in the same book when it came to handling some situations. It's worth sticking it out, as marriage gets better with age—like fine wine, I guess. Our retirement life is perfect. This is a stress-free time in our lives compared to some of those years working and raising you kids. We now do what we want when we want and don't have to worry about where we will get the money. Your mom likes working part-time. I like playing golf and having a beer with the guys in the club bar. We both volunteer at Kettering Hospital. Dottie can spend what she wants without worrying about keeping to a budget. But you know your mom; she isn't going to pay full price for anything. She gets a generous discount at the boutique," her dad said, rolling his eyes with a wry grin.

"Dad, I'm happy for the two of you. I hope David and I can be in the same place when we get older and past our stressful situations."

"Are you saying you and David are having problems?"

"Our business can be demanding, and we disagree on how some matters should be handled. Hopefully, it's just a marital bump in the road, and we will be able to work out our problems."

She didn't want to tell her parents she and David were having serious problems. Her parents' peaceful life was about to be shaken by what would seem like a 7.5-magnitude earthquake when they learned interest in Edward Werner's death had resurfaced. Now was not the time to lay additional worries on them with her marital problem. The truth was two weeks ago David had rented a one-bedroom apartment close to his office, and he spent most nights there. His justification was that he could work late and get to the office earlier by not having to make the hour-long drive to and from their condo. Penelope suspected there was another reason. She wouldn't be surprised if divorce papers were waiting for her when she returned to Denver.

"All marriages have rough patches. I'm sure you and David will resolve your problems. Now let's get some coffee cake," her dad said.

"I'm on it, Dad."

Her mother entered the kitchen, makeup on, hair in place, but still in her robe. "I'm sorry, Pen. I need to go to work today. One of the girls had a family emergency. I had hoped to be off while you were here, but Cynthia was almost in tears when she called. They have an ad in the paper today promoting a preholiday sale. She needs my help. I couldn't turn her down."

"Mom, don't worry about it. I have a few things I need to do and calls to make." Penelope was glad to have the day to herself. It would give her time to sort out how to handle Elizabeth, considering what she'd learned from reading the journal. "Why don't I take you to work? Then I can use your car to do my running around. Dad and I can pick you up at six, and we can have dinner at one of the new restaurants you were telling me about."

"Thanks, dear, that sounds perfect. We need to leave here by nine thirty."

1

AFTER DROPPING HER mom off at the boutique, Penelope returned home to make some calls. First, she called the downtown library's archive department to speak to Reed Remington, the college student who had researched Edward Werner for her. She wanted to thank him in person for his quick response to her requests.

After several rings, the call was answered. "Hello, is this Reed Remington?'

"Yes, this is Reed."

"Reed, this is Penelope Parker. We spoke a couple weeks ago. You did research for me on—"

"Yes, I remember," he interrupted. "You wanted information on a man, Edward Werner, as I recall."

"You have a good memory," Penelope replied. "I'm in Dayton and would like to stop by the library to thank you in person. How long will you be working today?"

"I'll be here till three today. Come on down anytime."

"Great! I will be there between two and two thirty, if that works for you. It has been years since I have been in the downtown library. Are the archives still in the basement? Or the dungeon, as we called it when I was in high school."

"Afraid so, but it looks a little better. They painted the gray walls a bright color and installed better lighting. Plus, they got rid of all the dragons and torture chambers," Reed joked.

"Well, that's good news. I won't have to bring along my saber to fight off any dragons. See you this afternoon."

"I'll look forward to it. Bye now."

Before heading to the library, Penelope drove by the grade school and high school she'd attended. The trip down memory lane took her past several of her former friends' homes and the drive-in restaurant that had been a favorite hangout in high school. The old movie theatres were now boarded up or torn down. On the spur of the moment, she took a turn and drove by the house where she'd lived the first eighteen years of her life. Penelope had not been on the street since her parents moved to the suburbs over twenty-five years ago. The part of town where she grew up had changed dramatically. Many areas were not safe, especially for a woman alone. Her street was no exception. Cars were parked on both sides of the street, many with fenders missing or other parts damaged from accidents. Speed bumps were now on most streets. Yards overgrown with weeds and houses in need of paint and repairs were common. She was pleased to see her former home looked well maintained. The top of a playground swing set was visible over the wood fence in the backyard. No one fenced their yards in the years she had lived there. Now, many of the houses had fences—fences to keep people out and memories locked in, Penelope envisioned.

Penelope found a metered parking place in front of the library. She took the steps down to the basement and, pushing the door open to the archive department, she noticed a tall man about her age walking from a room in back. "I'm looking for Reed Remington," she inquired of the man.

"I'm Reed Remington. You must be Penelope Parker?"

She felt the heat rise from her neck upward, registering a surprised look. "Um, yes, I'm Penelope."

A wide grin spread across his face as he extended his hand to hers in a warm handshake. "Are you all right? You look like you were expecting to see a medieval dungeon keeper."

Penelope was now smiling with amusement. "No, not a dungeon keeper, but I was expecting a college student in his twenties."

"I am a college student. I guess you could say I'm a late bloomer. Come, let's sit down. There are two comfortable chairs next to the counter. I'll give you the five-minute recap of how an old guy became a college student."

After they were seated, Reed began. "My college education got delayed by Uncle Sam. I graduated from high school in 1968 (the year after she graduated). My parents were paying for my older brother's college tuition. They didn't have enough money left for me to go to college right after high school. I was able to get a full-time job in the factory at National Cash Register, or NCR, as it's commonly called. Living with my parents allowed me to save money for college, but my college plans got interrupted in August 1971 when my draft number came up. I was off to boot camp and from there to Vietnam for a year. I completed the remainder of my service at Fort Rucker Army Base in Alabama. I was twenty-three when I was discharged and didn't have a clue what I wanted to do with my life. I lost interest in going to college. After a couple of months of trying to figure what to do with my life, I went back to work for NCR. They had an excellent training program for individuals they considered to have potential for advancement. I eventually became a supervisor in one of the manufacturing departments. I started taking college classes at night but soon realized at that pace, I would be retirement age by the time I graduated. Two years ago, I left NCR to be a full-time student. I'll be a forty-four-year-old college graduate next month."

"Good for you. It's never too late to get an education. What do you plan to do with your degree in journalism?"

"That's a story for another time. What brings you to Dayton?" Reed asked.

"My parents and my brother and his family live south of Dayton in Centerville. I'm here for a two-week visit."

"I see. I thought maybe your trip was in connection with the information you requested on Edward Werner. Your request intrigued me and sparked my journalistic curiosity."

Penelope wasn't sure she wanted to carry the conversation about Werner any further. Remembering her purpose was to thank Reed, she avoided the subject by handing him the box of cookies she had purchased on her way downtown.

"I want to give you this box of cookies as a thank-you for helping me with my research. I was operating under the assumption you were a twenty-year-old living with some buddies in an apartment existing on a diet of beer and pizza, so I figured fresh-baked cookies from Cheryl's Bakery would be a welcome treat. Now I realize a bottle of wine would have been more appropriate."

"Not at all. The cookies are greatly appreciated, and my roommate, Charlie, will really enjoy them."

"Charlie?"

"Charlie is my four-legged roommate, a golden retriever

who loves food and people, in that order. Before Charlie gets his jaws on them, why don't we go to the cafe across the street for a cup of coffee and enjoy some of these delicious looking cookies ourselves? Maybe I will be able to entice you to reveal your interest in Edward Werner."

8

ENTICE HER? HE didn't need to entice her. She started babbling as though she were in a confessional booth before they even entered the coffee shop. Over an hour later, her eyes dropped to look at her watch. She needed to leave.

Driving home, Penelope shook her head in disbelief. She had revealed to a complete stranger her darkest secret, one she had never told anyone except her mother. She didn't divulge the vulgar details of her encounter with Werner, but he got the picture. Reed listened, asking appropriate questions but not prying. It amazed her how comfortable she felt talking to him.

Reed had given her some good advice. "Tell your parents about Elizabeth's letter. Ask them what they knew about Werner's death, but don't mention reading your mother's journal," he'd suggested. He also pointed out that knowing what was in the journal would give her the ability to ask leading questions.

Penelope's plan was for her and her parents to have a pleasant dinner at a new restaurant. When they returned home, she and her mom would change into comfortable clothes, most likely their gowns and robes. Her dad would be in his recliner, sipping a brandy and flipping through the TV channels. She would gather her parents in the den, telling them she had something to discuss. They would be curious to hear what she had to say, hoping it was good news.

Everything went as planned with dinner, and as her dad drove into the garage, right on cue, Dottie announced, "It was a lovely meal. Now, I am going to get on my gown and robe, sit by the fire, read my book, and toddle off to bed before ten. After all, I'm the only one who brought home the bacon today. You retiree and vacationer had a leisurely day while I was trying to put a size-sixteen lady into a size-twelve dress, which she insisted was her size."

They laughed as they watched Dottie go to the bedroom, waving her hand in a circular motion and swinging her hips.

A big grin crossed her dad's face. "Your mom keeps my life fun and entertaining."

"I'll get into my jammies too. I have something I want to talk to you and Mom about. Get your brandy, and I'll see you in the den in a few minutes." Penelope headed to the bedroom, waving and swinging her hips, imitating her mom.

Fifteen minutes later all three were in the den. The TV was off. Walt had his brandy, and Dottie had a book in her lap. Penelope was enjoying the smell of the wood burning in the fireplace as she entered the room. The crackling sound of the wood as the flames reached out to each log put a smile on her face. Nothing reminded Penelope more of her childhood than the sound, smell, and sight of a wood-burning fireplace. A few years ago, her mother had advocated to have gas logs installed, but her dad said as long as he was able to haul the wood in from their storage shed, they would have a wood-burning fireplace. Penelope was glad her dad had won that dispute.

Penelope sat on the sofa facing her parents. Her

nerves were on edge. She was chewing the lipstick off of her bottom lip. This was a conversation she dreaded, not only because it would be upsetting for her parents but because she feared what she might learn.

"So, what do you have to tell us? Your dad and I are all ears."

Penelope took a deep breath. There was no way to sugarcoat it. She had to jump right in. "I want to ask you about something that happened thirty-six years ago, in 1957." She looked at her parents to see their reaction. Her mother slowly moved her book from her lap to the table as her dad took a sip of brandy. Her parents glanced at each other, their eyes not meeting Penelope's.

"I'm sure you remember the summer of 1957. I doubt that summer has been totally forgotten by any of us. I never thought years later I would have to relive the experience. But that changed three weeks ago when I received a letter from Elizabeth Werner Scott." Penelope removed the letter from her pocket. Her hands were trembling as she began to read.

When she finished, her mother opened her mouth as though she was going to speak, but the words were stuck. When no sound was forthcoming, she exhaled a barely audible, "Oh, my." Penelope saw worry flash across her mother's face. Her mother took a tissue from her robe pocket and began twisting it around and around, her typical reaction when upset or worried.

Her dad took control. "What is it you want to know?" His voice was abrupt and commanding.

"I want you to tell me everything you know about Werner's death, all the details, and don't leave anything out. You can start with what you did when Mom told you what Werner had done to me."

"What makes you think I told him? You made me promise not to tell your father, remember?" her mom asked, indignant at the insinuation she had broken her promise.

"Come on, Mom. I'm an adult now, not a frightened eight-year-old child. I know you could not keep what happened to me from Dad. I expect you told him right after I told you. It's what parents do when something traumatic happens to their child."

Her dad had become agitated. He held up his hands to stop any further conversation between his wife and daughter. "Okay, okay, of course she told me, and I did what any father would do. At first, I wanted to confront Werner, but instead I went to Charles Taylor, a neighbor who was a detective with the Dayton police. The police took Werner in for questioning, and, as expected, he denied everything. The police didn't believe him, but there wasn't much they were able to do unless we filed a formal complaint, which would've required you to tell your story to the police. At the time, we weren't willing to put you through an interrogation and possibly having you repeat it in court. A short time later, it happened to another girl in the neighborhood, Joyce Mueller. You may remember her. After meeting with her father, we decided to file formal complaints with the police. A time was being scheduled with a child abuse specialist to interview you and the police were putting together their case. Werner would soon be arrested. He and his wife moved from the neighborhood, and a short time later he was found dead on an abandoned road. Werner opted to take the easy way out and killed himself before he was arrested."

"How did you learn of his death?" Penelope asked.

"Detective Taylor called me, and later we saw it in the paper."

Pressing her dad for more information, Penelope asked, "Did they question you and Mr. Mueller about his death?"

"Um, well, it was ruled a suicide. Foul play wasn't suspected." Her dad took another sip of brandy. Penelope shifted uncomfortably, crossing and uncrossing her legs. She didn't want to anger her dad, but she needed to know more. "Dad, I read the newspaper article from 1957 when his body was found. It stated his death was ruled a suicide but also stated that no note was found. Elizabeth's letter stated the medical examiner's report ruled suicide but said that suicide could not be 100 percent determined. The police would have done an investigation in order to rule out a possible homicide. If there was any hint of murder, you and John Mueller would have been prime suspects. The police must have questioned you both."

"Yes, they questioned both of us. Neither of us had anything to do with his death. John Mueller had been on the road for three days during the time of Werner's death, and I was at work or home in the time period they were investigating. The police verified our alibis. We were never considered suspects in a murder. We were only questioned because we had registered complaints against Werner. Werner's family members and work associates were also questioned. Everyone was cleared. The gun belonged to Werner. His fingerprints were the only ones found on the weapon. Except for the farmer who found Werner dead in his car, there were no other tire tracks or footprints on the road. The police concluded Werner realized it was only a matter of time before he was arrested charged with being a pedophile. He took his own life to save himself and his family from the humiliation. I hope this satisfies the matter for you."

Her dad's jaw tightened as he pressed his lips together in a thin line, his arms folded across this chest. She knew the look.

"Dad, please understand that in no way do I think you had anything to do with Werner's death."

"Well, I certainly hope not."

"I just needed to know the facts before I contact Elizabeth," Penelope explained.

"Contact Elizabeth? Why would you contact her?" Her mother exclaimed. "Let her remember her grandfather the way she knew him. You'll be opening a can of worms if you talk to her!"

"Elizabeth will not let this go. I need to tell her what kind of man her grandfather was. If I don't, I can guarantee she will knock on your door one day. Let's hope when she learns about her grandfather's background, she will stop searching for answers." Penelope said trying to justify her reason to contact Elizabeth.

"I don't like this one bit—not one bit! So when do you plan to do this noble deed?" her mother asked with a questioning sneer.

Surprised by her mom's reaction, Penelope went on. "I'm sorry, Mom. I don't like it either. I didn't like living it thirty-six years ago, and I don't like reliving it now. Why are you opposed to my talking to Elizabeth? Dad isn't objecting. Should I be asking you what you know about Werner's death? You had to be enraged when I told you what he had done."

"Of course, I was enraged—your father and I both were. John Mueller even threated to castrate him. But we are not vigilantes." Her mom was now on the verge of tears. "There is something more Werner did which your dad didn't mention. Do you remember going to Grandma and Pop Evans in Glenville for the rest of the summer? Werner found out you were in West Virginia and he drove to Glenville. Pop saw him drive by their house three times one weekend. On Sunday, Werner was sitting in his car when you came out of church. Pop got his license plate, and your dad had the police check to be sure the car belonged to Werner, which it did. When I heard that, I feared Werner may have been planning to kidnap and kill you as he promised he would. It was the worst nightmare of my life—our lives. When I learned he was dead, I was ecstatic with joy. I didn't care how he had died. If he had been murdered and I found out who did it, I would have thrown them a party. I would have done whatever possible to keep the murderer from going to prison. Do I know anything about his death? No, I don't!" Upset and in tears, she got up from her chair and left the room.

Her father stood. "Pen, do what you want about Elizabeth. I agree, Elizabeth is looking for answers, and she's not likely to stop until she knows the truth about her grandfather. Talk to me first before you bring it up again with your mother. Now, I need to go comfort my wife." Giving his daughter a tender pat on her shoulder, he walked to the back bedroom.

In the morning, Penelope would try to smooth things over with her mother. Seeing her mom upset distressed her, but she would not change her mind about contacting Elizabeth. Walking to the kitchen, she heard her mother before she saw her.

"Here, read this," her mother said, tossing the journal Penelope had just read that morning, on the counter.

"What's this?" Penelope stammered, trying not to register a guilty look.

"It's my daily journal beginning the day you told me what happened. You want to know all the details. Well, here are the details. I hope this will help you understand what your father and I went through. It may have been the wrong decision not to tell you Werner was dead. You were only eight. As parents we were trying to protect you. We didn't want to keep bringing up his name. We wanted you to go on like it hadn't happened."

Dottie Evans was from the stiff-upper-lip generation. Her approach was to handle unpleasant situations as best you could, then put the memories in a box, and seal it tight. Don't discuss it again and go on like it never happened.

"That's the problem, Mom. It did happen. Those memories didn't go away because you didn't want to talk about it."

"I know, honey. I'm sorry. Read this and then we can talk." Dottie handed the journal to Penelope.

"I'll read it tonight. Mom, I'm sorry I upset you. I didn't want our visit to be like this."

"I know. It's not your fault. Elizabeth is the one pushing to find answers. Call her tomorrow. Meet with her. Tell her about her grandfather, and, if she questions your story, show her this journal."

9

THE NEXT MORNING Penelope called Elizabeth's office number. The receptionist told her Elizabeth was not in the office but would be there within the hour. Penelope left a message. Twenty minutes later Elizabeth called.

"Penelope, this is Elizabeth. I'm glad you called. I hope we can get together and catch up on..."

Penelope cut her off in midsentence. This was not a social call for her. She wanted to avoid idle chit-chat and get to the point. "Elizabeth, I'll meet you either today or tomorrow morning to discuss the topic you seem to have become so interested in. What is your schedule?"

"I can meet you for lunch either day or any other time convenient for you."

"Lunch is not possible. Can you meet in an hour for coffee at Doug's Doughnuts near downtown on Brown Street?"

"I'll be there. I hope we will recognize each other." Elizabeth's voice was cheerful with the anticipation of seeing an old friend.

"I'll be at the small booth in the back next to the window. See you at nine-thirty." There was an edge to her voice as Penelope abruptly hung up.

Meet for lunch—was she kidding? The idea of discussing Edward Werner over a chicken salad sandwich was the last thing Penelope was interested in doing. No doubt Elizabeth was looking forward to a pleasant reunion. Elizabeth had no idea what she was about to learn. Penelope hoped Elizabeth would not get emotional. Seeing tears shed for such an evil man would be more than she could take. Elizabeth was an investigator for the police department. She would have seen and heard worse things. She would know people were not always what they appeared to be, though it was sure to be different when it was someone you had loved.

Before leaving to meet Elizabeth, Penelope called Doug, her high school friend, who owned Doug's Doughnuts. She told him she was meeting a woman there at nine-thirty and asked him to put a reserved sign on the small table in the back. She said she planned to arrive by nine.

Her dad's golf buddies had picked him up, leaving his car for her. Her mom was in the bedroom getting dressed. Penelope left a note on the kitchen counter to let her mom know she was meeting Elizabeth. Clutching her envelope-style briefcase, with her mother's journal secured inside, she started to the garage just as her mother walked out of the kitchen.

"I saw your note. This won't be easy for either of you. It will be upsetting for Elizabeth. I hope she doesn't cause you any problems. Hopefully, you won't need to show her my journal, but if you do, don't let her take it to read."

"No, Mom, I won't allow her to take the journal. If Elizabeth doesn't believe what I tell her, then I will show her your journal. She won't be able to read it all, but she will read enough to know what I told her is the truth. I'll call you from Doug's after I meet with her. It may be an hour or more, so don't worry."

"Me, worry? The queen of worry, who can make bigger mountains out of molehills than anyone?" her mother said with a sheepish half smile.

"But this ain't no molehill, Mom," Penelope replied, giving her mother a hug.

10

PENELOPE ENTERED DOUG'S Doughnuts shortly before nine. Doug greeted her with a hug. He always smelled yummy, like a mixture of spices. Today it was cinnamon, chocolate, and a hint of nutmeg. Anytime she was in town, Penelope made it a point to visit Doug. He would take time out of the kitchen to enjoy a cup of coffee with her while they caught up on old friends.

"Who are you meeting here today? Anyone I know?" he inquired.

"I doubt if you know her. She's not one of our classmates. We were friends when we were seven and eight years old. Actually, this is not a social visit. I have some unpleasant business to discuss with her, which is why I wanted the booth in the back. Thanks for reserving it for me. She should arrive at nine thirty, and I have no idea what she looks like. Her name is Elizabeth, in case you see a woman my age looking around."

"I got it. I am not to bother you with my usual charming personality."

"Right, unless you have to break up a fight. I'm kidding. It's not that kind of meeting. More apt to be tears instead of spears. I'll talk to you before I leave and get my usual box of doughnuts to take home."

Doug handed her a mug of coffee and gave her a pat on the shoulder as he headed back to the kitchen. "Holler if you need me."

Penelope walked to the booth, taking the side facing the door. Doug had placed spoons on two cloth napkins along with a plate of assorted doughnut holes, a carafe of coffee, and a coffee mug for her guest. Doug's may be merely a doughnut shop, but no paper napkins, cups, or plastic utensils were ever used. Drinking out of paper cups and using plastic was not the way to start your day, according to Doug. The coffee mugs were colorful. Many were from various places he had traveled. Friends brought him mugs from their travels and memorable events they attended. It was fun to see what mug you were served. Doug often entertained customers with a humorous narrative on the history of a particular mug.

Doug wanted his customers to have a relaxing and pleasing atmosphere. The walls were painted in soft colors, with artwork displayed by local artists. A fresh floral arrangement adorned the counter. Glass bud vases with seasonal flowers were on each table—no plastic flowers for Doug. It helped that he was part owner of the flower shop next door. The booth benches were padded, and all the chairs had colorful cushions. Between seven and nine on weekday mornings, people had to wait for a place to park. Customers lined up to purchase boxes of doughnuts to take to coworkers or to get coffee and a doughnut to go. Penelope knew the workers would be gone by nine thirty, replaced by retirees or couples starting their day at Doug's.

Promptly at nine-thirty, an attractive, slender woman walked in, looking from one side of the room to the other. She was dressed in slacks and a matching blazer. Penelope was thankful Elizabeth wasn't wearing a police uniform, as she had feared she might. Penelope stood up and waved to her. Elizabeth's face brightened with a friendly smile, and she picked up her pace to greet her long-ago friend. She approached Penelope as though she was going to give her a hug, but Penelope quickly extended her hand. This was not an embracing occasion for her. "Hello, Elizabeth," she said, sitting down and motioning for Elizabeth to take the seat across from her.

Elizabeth relaxed as she slid into the booth. "I have passed by here many times but never stopped in. It's charming."

"Yes, it is. A high school friend of mine owns it. Doug's coffee and doughnuts are the best in town. Please, help yourself to the coffee and doughnut holes."

Penelope cleared her throat. "I think we should forgo any small talk and get right to the reason we are here. You're on a mission to learn more about your grandfather's death, to determine whether he committed suicide or was murdered. For some reason, after thirty-six years, you now have become compelled to dig into it. I will tell you the truth about your grandfather, but you are not going to like what I tell you. I wish you would let the memory you have of your grandfather remain the way you remembered him. But you, Elizabeth, are the one who has brought this on—not me."

Penelope realized her tone and manner had been harsh to the point of being rude. Uncrossing her arms and placing her folded hands on the table as though in prayer, she softened her voice.

She started with the birthday party and going to Elizabeth's grandparents' house the next day. Penelope told how her grandfather had enticed her into the basement with the movies and sexually abused her. She didn't go into the sordid details of the experience. Penelope mentioned Joyce Mueller's experience and said that both Mr. Mueller and her father had reported the incidents to the police.

She went on about the police taking him in for questioning several times and her grandfather's continual denial of the accusations, adding that the police didn't believe him.

Elizabeth's relaxed demeanor changed, her friendly smile vanished, and her back stiffened. She wrapped both hands around her coffee mug as though the mug was giving her stability to keep her from falling. Shaking her head in disbelief, she said, "I find this very hard to believe. But, if this is true, which I have serious doubts it is, then someone may have had a motive to kill my grandfather."

"I can assure you it is the truth. Your grandfather even threatened to kill me if I told anyone. The next day, I told my mom. I begged her not to tell my dad, but of course she did. Last night, I talked to my parents and read them the letter you sent. I learned for the first time that the police had been involved and about Joyce Mueller's experience. My parents and the Muellers were both distraught over what happened to their daughters. Complaints were filed with the police. When your grandfather was found dead, my father and John Mueller were questioned along with other neighbors, work associates, and your family members. Mr. Mueller was a truck driver and had been on the road the week of the incident. My dad was at work or home during that week. Their statements were confirmed by their employers, their wives, and their neighbors. The gun belonged to your grandfather; his were the only fingerprints on it. He had to know he would soon be arrested and convicted as a pedophile. You should be grateful that he had the decency to save you and your family from the disgrace and humiliation of a public trial."

Elizabeth learned forward, her eyes focused on Penelope, and with confidence stated, "I don't think you can say a conviction was a sure thing. From what you have told me, the only testimony would be from an eight-year-old girl and a ten-year-old girl. My grandfather may have given you girls a hug, a kiss on the cheek, or a pat on the leg, and you girls misinterpreted the gesture."

Penelope's mouth dropped open and, with a look of indignation, said, "Are you suggesting I'm making this up? What reason would I have?"

"No, I'm not saying you are making it up. But I know young girls have active imaginations, and as I recall you had a very active one. Playing make-believe was one of your favorite activities. Over time, you may be recalling the incident worse than what it really was. I want to read the reports for myself."

"For heaven sakes, Elizabeth! What young child doesn't play make-believe? I can assure you, I have a vivid memory of what he did, and it was not an insignificant gesture which was misinterpreted, as you suggest. Get the police reports. You'll find a detailed, handwritten statement by Joyce Mueller. You'll learn he was stalking me when I was visiting my grandparents in Glenville, West Virginia. You will find out how ..."

"Wait a minute!" Elizabeth interrupted. "We had family near Glenville. It wouldn't have been unusual for my grandfather to be there. And what do you mean he was stalking you?"

"I know you had family in the area, but they lived nowhere close to my grandparents' home. He had no reason to be driving around their neighborhood or parked outside their church on a Sunday when I was there with my grandparents."

A smirk formed on Elizabeth's lips. She rolled her eyes, giving a skeptical look. Penelope felt her blood begin to boil; she'd like to slap that smirk off her face. Penelope reached for her briefcase and took the envelope out.

"I wish I didn't have to show you this, but you seem to need more concrete proof. My mother has kept a diary every day of her life since she was in her teens. When I told my mom what your grandfather did, she started keeping a detailed journal in a notebook instead of briefer daily entries in her diary. I suppose she felt the need to journal to help her deal with what happened and, to also have an accurate account in case Werner was brought to trial or, worse, in the event he kept his promise and murdered me.

"I read this journal for the first time yesterday. Before then, I didn't know the police were involved or about Joyce Mueller's experience. All these years, I assumed my mom was the only person who knew, and we never talked about it again. I presume my parents were trying to shelter me by not mentioning it. I was already terrified by his threat to kill me. If I had known my dad knew and he had gone to the police, I would never have wanted to leave the house."

Penelope poured herself another cup of coffee and picked up a doughnut piece. She studied Elizabeth as she was reading the journal. When they'd been children, Elizabeth's hair had been dark and curly; it was cut short and worn with colorful headbands. Her dark hair now was shoulder length and straight, no doubt due to all the new hair-straightening techniques. Penelope pictured Elizabeth toiling away with a flat iron to battle the curls every morning while Penelope was trying to curl hers.

As kids, they were together almost daily during the summer. Elizabeth's skin was always tanned. Now in early November, she still had the same tan. Her skin had a velvety caramel tone. She was a pretty woman. Thinking back, Penelope realized Elizabeth never talked about her father. She talked about her mother and Nellie, the girl who took care of her when her mother was working. Elizabeth's mother's last name was Werner. Evidently, her mother had not been married, or Elizabeth would have had a different last name. If her mother was divorced, she would have kept her married name. In the fifties, divorced women with children did not take back their maiden names.

Elizabeth looked up from the notebook. "This is an

interesting document. I'm not able to read it all now. Would you allow me to take it and get it back to you tomorrow?"

"I am sorry, but the journal belongs to my mother. I can't leave it with you without her permission. I doubt she will allow you or anyone to have the original, but I will ask her if I can make a copy for you. I'll let you know later today or tomorrow."

"Please, Penelope. I need to know all the facts, and your mother has important details in her journal."

"If my mom agrees to give you a copy, would it be possible for me to make the copy at your office?"

"Yes, no problem," Elizabeth replied. "I have flexible hours. Call me and I will meet you in my office at police headquarters. Do you know where we're located?"

"On West Third Street, right?"

"Yes, the visitor parking is in the back. The officer at the reception desk will let me know when you arrive, and I'll meet you in the lobby. Penelope, thanks for agreeing to meet with me today. I look forward to hearing from you tomorrow." Elizabeth slid out of the booth and strode out of the shop.

Penelope wasn't sure how her mother would feel about Elizabeth having a copy of the journal. Once a copy was made, it could get into anyone's hands, and she knew her mother would not want that to happen. Her mother was a fairly private person when it came to personal and family matters. They would have to give this careful consideration.

11

PENELOPE GAVE A sigh of relief that this initial meeting was over. She gathered up the journal and went to look for Doug. He was coming out of the kitchen as she approached the counter.

"How did your meeting go?" Doug asked, setting a tray of doughnuts on the counter.

"No bloodshed, but we have unfinished business. I need to make a couple of calls. May I use the phone in your office?"

"Better yet, use the phone upstairs in my apartment. It can get noisy outside my office with the kitchen staff banging pots and pans around. The door is unlocked. There are phones in the kitchen, bedroom, and living room—take your pick and take your time. I'll see you before you leave."

Doug had moved to the space above the shop several years ago. He decided it was foolish to pay rent on an apartment in downtown Dayton when he owned a building with adequate room above his shop. He renovated the space, turning it into a delightful two-bedroom, two-bath apartment. A mahogany bar divided the kitchen from the dining and living area. The master bedroom had an alcove with a floor-to-ceiling bookcase full of books and memorabilia. A comfortable reading chair with a table lamp sat in front of a window. The sun filtering through the trees gave the cozy alcove a relaxing warmth. Penelope wished she could curl up in the chair with a good book and stay all day.

She used the phone in the living room to call home, knowing her mom would be waiting to hear how the meeting with Elizabeth had gone. She gave her mother a brief recap along with Elizabeth's request to have a copy of the journal. They decided to discuss it at dinner along with her dad.

Her next call was to Reed. She felt she needed to fill him in on her "intriguing situation," as he called it. His advice had helped her decide how to approach her parents. He had written his phone number on an old library catalog card, telling her he hoped she would call because he was interested in learning how "it all plays out." Digging in her purse, she found the card and dialed the number. To her surprise, he answered on the second ring. After a brief conversation, he suggested they meet for lunch. They agreed to meet at Marion's Pizza in an hour.

Penelope freshened up in Doug's bathroom, went downstairs to thank Doug, and picked up a box of doughnuts. She promised to stop by or at least call him before she left town.

———◆◆◆———

Reed was already at Marion's when she arrived. When she met him at the library, he'd had a day-old beard, but today he was clean shaven. He wore khaki pants with a light blue dress shirt under a royal blue V-neck sweater. The combination made his ice-blue eyes sparkle. She could get lost in those blue eyes. His dark hair had a touch of gray beginning to peek out around his temples. She guessed his height to be six feet or six one. His engaging smile had made her instantly like him when they first met, and she was no less charmed by it now. She felt a little uneasy meeting him for lunch. Lunching with a man was not uncommon for Penelope, but since she'd been married, they had been work associates or old friends. This felt different.

Reed stood up and greeted her with a two-handed handshake. Pulling out her chair, he said, "I ordered a pizza, half pepperoni and half with everything. I hope one or both will suit your palate."

"Perfect, I like both."

"Great! I'll get the drinks. What would you like?"

"Diet Pepsi will be fine. Thank you," Penelope replied, sliding off her jacket.

Reed returned to the table with the pizza and drinks. Settling in the chair across from her and taking a square of pizza he began, "So, you met with Elizabeth?"

"I did. I met with her this morning. First, I want to thank you for letting me vent the other day. It helped me decide how to proceed. I talked to my parents. They were stunned to learn Elizabeth had contacted me all these years later. They told me what they remembered about Werner's death. It wasn't a pleasant conversation. My mom was upset and against my contacting Elizabeth. Later she gave me her journal instructing me to show it to Elizabeth if she doubted what I told her about her grandfather. This morning, I called Elizabeth and we met at Doug's Doughnuts."

"Doug's is one of my favorite places. Doug and I are friends; we play racquetball together."

"Really? Doug and I are old friends. We went to high school together. I make a point to get together with him when I'm in town. How did you meet him?"

"We met at the racquetball court a few years ago. A lot of the guys who play are younger and faster. Doug and I realized we were about the same age and evenly matched. He wins some, I win some, and we have a good time playing together. On a few occasions, we've gone out for a beer or grabbed a bite after a rigorous game. But enough about Doug—let's get back to your meeting with Elizabeth. How did she respond to the news about her grandfather?"

"After our awkward greeting, I gave her the ugly truth about her grandfather. As you can imagine, she was shocked and appalled. She didn't want to accept the truth, implying it was the imagination of two young girls. I had to show her the journal to convince her. She read a few pages and asked to take the journal so she could finish reading it. I wasn't able to let her take it, but I'll ask my mom if I can make a copy for her. So that's where it stands. I'll talk to my mom tonight and let Elizabeth know in the next day or two. I'm hoping she will drop the matter after she reads the entire journal."

Penelope reached for her drink. "Let's talk about something else. I need to get my mind off the Werners. Tell me, what do you plan to do when you become 'The Graduate' next month?"

"I guess I will have to find Mrs. Robinson," Reed said with a devilish grin. "Actually, I do have a plan. In the beginning, journalism was my major. I wanted to write and was interested in investigative reporting. It's a difficult field to get into, I soon learned. I should have started in my twenties. I've written a few articles for magazines and will continue to write. My other interest is history. My degree will be in history with a minor in journalism. I plan to teach high school history and creative writing. I've interviewed with three schools and have one more scheduled after Thanksgiving. The feedback has been positive. To my advantage, my age and life experiences appear to be a plus."

"Absolutely they are a plus. You'll make a fine teacher.

I was a fourth-grade substitute teacher for a short time in Colorado. The teacher was on maternity leave for six months. I had time to get to know the students and observed their progress. It was a rewarding experience. The last day of school before the summer break, the students wrote me thank-you notes. I still have them."

"Why didn't you stay with teaching?"

"After I graduated from college, I substitute taught for income until I went back to school for my master's in social work. I finished my master's, married, and began working with my husband to build his law practice. Now that his law practice is doing well, I hope to utilize my MSW. I'm not sure what area I want to pursue in the social work field. In Denver I do home studies for couples who are adopting children. My cases are mostly older children who are being adopted by grandparents, a stepparent, or some other family member. Whatever I do, it will be working with or for the benefit of children."

"Sounds like you have your career path mapped out. Now, tell me something about Penelope Parker that most people don't know," Reed asked, raising his eyebrows with an inquisitive look.

"Hmm. Well, let's see, I'm a wicked chess player. I talk in my sleep, mostly about food. I got my first kiss in the sixth grade and have liked kissing ever since," Penelope stated with a coy smile. "Now back at you, Mr. Reed Remington. Surprise me with some little-known facts about you."

Reed gave her a mischievous smile, a hint she was about to learn something no one else knew. He placed his right hand with folded fingers under his chin and his left hand on his leg posing like *The Thinker.* "I rock at solitaire. I walk in my sleep, generally to the refrigerator to get a beer. I kissed a girl in the fifth grade. She slapped my face, and I haven't kissed a girl since."

Both had been trying not to laugh, but now they

could not contain themselves. Tears were rolling down Penelope's cheeks. He winked at her as he handed his handkerchief to dry her eyes.

What is it about a wink? She thought. An unattractive man can give you a personal wink and somehow you find him appealing. The wink from Reed, coupled with his captivating blue eyes, made her tingle from her head to her toes. "Thank you for the hankie." She flashed him a demure look with her thick-lashed brown eyes. His eyes held hers. With a sexy half-smile and alluring gaze, he said, "Happy to help." It was like they were having eye foreplay.

12

PENELOPE COULD NOT remember the last time she had flirted with anyone. Marriage somehow ended flirting. What a shame.

On her way home, Penelope replayed the lunch with Reed. A smile spread across her face as she thought about their conversation. Being with Reed felt natural and comfortable. This confused her. Was it because her relationship with her husband was falling apart? Was she craving male companionship, someone to listen and understand her bizarre predicament? Or was there more to her feelings? Regardless, she needed a confidant, and Reed had drawn the short straw.

Turning onto Main Street, she stopped at Radio Shack. Several of her friends in Denver had purchased mobile phones and commented on how useful they were. She had planned on getting one when she returned to Denver but decided now was a good time to learn more about these new devices. An hour later, Penelope walked out of the store with a purse-sized handheld Nokia 1011 cellular phone. She would charge the phone overnight. To start with, she'd give her new phone number to her parents, her brother, David, Elizabeth, Reed, and a few friends.

When she arrived home, her mother was in the kitchen preparing dinner. Her dad was napping in his chair in the den. The aroma of her mom's pot roast was wafting through the house. On the kitchen counter was an envelope from David. After changing her clothes, she opened the envelope. Divorce papers fell to the floor. A note was attached.

> *Penelope, neither of us has been happy for some time. I think we both need to move on with our lives. I have tried to be generous and fair regarding our joint property. Call when you want to discuss further. David*

She briefly flipped through the document and stuck it in a drawer. Her emotions were a mix of anger, sadness, disappointment, and maybe a bit of relief. But she had too much to deal with at the moment to let those emotions take over her thoughts. She would read the document later when she had the time to review it in detail and talk to David.

Over a somber dinner, Penelope recounted the details of the meeting with Elizabeth. Her dad had never read the journal and asked to read it before any decision was made on giving Elizabeth a copy.

Later in the evening, after he'd read the journal, the three of them gathered around the kitchen table. Her dad spoke first., "I don't think a copy of the journal should be given to Elizabeth. Your mom was under a lot of fearful stress during that summer. There are statements that could be misconstrued and incriminating for us, as well as for John Mueller." He went on to say, "You can tell Elizabeth your mom is not comfortable sharing the personal and private thoughts she recorded during a very distressing time. Answer her questions, but for now I think the journal needs to be kept in our hands."

Penelope looked from her father to her mother and nodded in agreement. He was right. The journal needed to stay private. "I don't think Elizabeth is going to be happy about this, but there is nothing she can do about it, at least not for now," Penelope said. "If she is successful in getting the case reopened, she can get a subpoena for the journal. Let's hope it doesn't go that far."

13

PENELOPE ARRIVED AT the police station the next morning having decided to break news of the no-go regarding the journal in person, though she didn't relish the thought of another awkward meeting with Elizabeth. She had, however, made up her mind to be friendlier on this meeting.

The three-story building was landscaped with evergreen shrubs and a few small trees. The reception area was sparse. The floor was an industrial gray tile with a lighter gray on the walls. There were no chairs, but several padded benches lined the walls. Around the room were pictures depicting the history of the Dayton Police Department. Dominating the reception area was a large, glass-enclosed cubicle where a female officer presided. Penelope gave the officer her name, stating she had an appointment with Elizabeth Scott.

Elizabeth entered the reception area a few minutes later, greeting Penelope cordially. "We can grab a cup of coffee in our breakroom. It's usually quiet there this time of day. I'm sure you would prefer the breakroom to an interrogation room?" Elizabeth smiled in her attempt at humor.

"The breakroom sounds fine. Lead the way," Penelope agreed, matching Elizabeth's smile and footsteps.

Walking in silence, they entered the breakroom, which was much more inviting than the entry area. It was painted a bright yellow and had windows that looked out to the side street. Several colorful posters adorned the walls. "You were right. It is quiet here—not a soul in sight," Penelope observed.

"Cops drink a lot of coffee, but they usually get it to go. The administrative staff uses it for their breaks and lunch. Since it's after ten, I don't think we'll be disturbed. Help yourself to coffee, tea, or if you prefer, there are soft drinks in the fridge."

Penelope poured a cup of coffee and took a seat near a window. "Elizabeth, my mother is not comfortable giving you a copy of her personal journal. It was written during a stressful and emotional time for her. She doesn't want to have a copy of it circulating in the hands of unknown people."

"I would be the only one reading it. I don't intend to show it to anyone else. In fact, I don't need a copy. I only want to read it. You can be with me while I read it."

"I'm sorry, but she was firm on not sharing it with anyone. She agreed I could show the journal to you yesterday if you needed confirmation that what I told you was the truth. You were able to read enough to know I was telling you the truth. If you have more questions, I will tell you what I know."

"I have a lot of unanswered questions, but I doubt you will be able to answer them."

"Elizabeth, I know how difficult this must be for you. I may have been snappy when we met yesterday. It was an uncomfortable situation for me, for both of us, and I apologize if I was rude. I understand you have a desire to learn the circumstances of your grandfather's death. On the other hand, I think from what you now know, your grandfather had a reason to commit suicide and the evidence supports suicide."

"That may be true, but there were some individuals who undoubtedly would have wanted to see him dead. I'm sure you realize it's a possibility."

"I don't know what more I can tell you. Are your mother and grandmother still alive? If so, can you question them?" Penelope asked.

"They are both alive and doing well. "Mom recently retired from the accounting firm where she worked for forty years. She loves sports and has an amazing knowledge of football, basketball, and baseball statistics. Now, she's beginning to get into soccer. She plays a lot of golf and, I am sure, knows the names of anyone who has ever held a club in their hand.

"Grandma is eighty-six. She lives in an assisted living facility in Brookville. Her mind is great, sharp as a tack, but her body is failing her. A year or so after Grandpa died, she went to work in a Hallmark gift shop. She'd never had a job before. She enjoyed interacting with people and made some friends. The experience was good for her. It gave her confidence and boosted her self-esteem."

"Do you see your mom and grandma often?"

"I talk to my mom every week. I try to visit Grandma once a month. It doesn't always work out with the boys' schedule and my work. I have never questioned her about Grandpa's death, and it has been many years since I discussed it with my mom. I have plans to visit Grandma later this week, and I intend to ask her about his death. I see Nellie or talk to her every few weeks. I doubt she will know anything unless she overheard something when Mom and Grandma were talking. I will ask her the next time we are together."

"I forgot about Nellie. I only met her once, but I remember you used to talk about her. Didn't she live with you and your mom?"

"Yes, she did. Mom worked, and Nellie took care of me and the house. She also did most of the grocery shopping and cooking. Nellie started cleaning my grandparents' house when she was in high school. When I was born, she moved in with us. It allowed my mom to work full-time, and I didn't have to grow up in a daycare. As a young child, I spent a great deal of time with Nellie. She took me to school and various activities. Nellie will always be special to me. She adores my sons. We consider her part of our family."

"Does she still live with your mom?"

"Oh, no. Nellie moved out after I graduated from high school. She worked cleaning houses and babysitting until she saved enough money to rent and furnish a small house on Rugby Road. For the past twenty-plus years she has worked in the cafeteria at a high school near her home. After Grandpa died, Grandma couldn't afford to continue to pay Nellie to clean her house, but by then, Grandma was dependent on Nellie. My mom arranged to pay her and started deducting social security from Nellie's check. Now, Nellie will be able to collect social security along with her retirement from the school district when she retires."

"Elizabeth, it may not be any of my business, but who was your father?"

Elizabeth wasn't sure she wanted to get into a conversation about her father—or lack of a father. She hesitated but then said, "I guess it's only fair for me to tell you a little about my private life since I'm asking you for personal details about yours. To be honest, I don't know who my father was. Over the years, I've asked my mom about my father, but she never wants to talk about it. She says she didn't know his name or she can't remember his name. It was a one-time thing after a party where they had been drinking. She had graduated from college with an accounting degree and was working part-time at Rike's

Department Store while looking for a full-time job with an accounting firm. I wasn't a big baby—I only weighed five pounds. Mom didn't gain much weight, which made it easy to keep her pregnancy a secret. She quit the job at Rike's a month before I was born. I think she was going to give me up for adoption, but my grandparents were against the adoption and suggested Nellie live with us. The arrangement worked well. Nellie had free room and board, Mom had her career, and instead of a mom and dad, I had two moms."

"It sounds like you have a good relationship with your family," Penelope observed. "How do you think they will respond when you tell them of your intent to find out more about your grandfather's death? Will you tell them what you learned from me and about my mom's journal?"

"I will have to tread lightly with that information. I don't want to upset my grandma by suggesting her husband was a pedophile, but I do plan to ask her about the circumstances of his death. My questions will depend on how willing she is to discuss the details of his death. She never talks about him, so it may be difficult."

"I hope you are able to get some answers and get this resolved. Elizabeth, I need to get going. I have another appointment. Thanks for the coffee."

They walked back to the reception area, making casual conversation. As Penelope was opening the door to leave, she remembered to give Elizabeth her mobile phone number.

Penelope had no idea what Elizabeth's grandmother would be able or willing to tell Elizabeth, but if anyone had the answers, it most likely was Mildred Werner.

14

PENELOPE'S PHONE RANG as she was preparing to meet her brother for lunch. It was Elizabeth. "I took your advice and talked to my grandma. I have some important new information disproving suicide. I need to talk to you. When and where do you want to meet?"

"My schedule is full the rest of the week. Go ahead and tell me over the phone."

"No, we need to talk in person. I can come to your parents' house later today. They need to hear what I have to say too."

"Elizabeth, that's not a good idea. This entire situation has already been upsetting enough for my parents. I'm here to enjoy time with my family, not to cause them undue stress." Penelope had made a sincere effort to be friendly and understanding when they met last week at the police station, but now, Elizabeth's demanding behavior was beginning to get on her nerves. "I will meet you at four today at Knapp's Restaurant on Far Hills," Penelope suggested.

"Fine, I'll be there."

They both pulled into the parking lot of Knapp's at the same time. Neither one was smiling. Elizabeth approached

Penelope as though she were going to handcuff her and read her the Miranda rights. Elizabeth was beginning to irritate Penelope.

With the exception of a waitress filling salt shakers, the restaurant was vacant, waiting for the early-bird diners to arrive. They took a table by the door and both ordered Cokes.

"So, Elizabeth, enlighten me. What is this riveting news that is so crucial you couldn't tell me over the phone?" Penelope leaned back in the chair, folding her arms across her chest.

"As I said, I visited Grandma. I asked her what she knew about Grandpa's death. Specifically, why did he take his own life? Without hesitating, she said he didn't kill himself. I was taken aback and asked her to explain. She went on to say the gunshot was to the right side of his head, but he was left-handed and couldn't have pulled the trigger with his right hand. When he was two or three years old, his right hand got shut in a car door. His right index finger was broken in several places, and he never was able to bend the finger. He could raise it up and down, but the joints didn't bend. The injury resulted in him becoming left-handed. He shot a rifle and a gun with his left hand when he was a young man. He did everything left handed."

"Interesting. It's apparent your grandmother didn't give the police this information. Why not? Why now?" Penelope inquired.

"I asked her the same question. She said the police never asked her. She read it on his death certificate."

"Why didn't she contact the police after she read the death certificate?"

"I don't know why. She shook her head when I asked her but never gave me an answer. I believe she may have known what you and Joyce Mueller alleged."

"Alleged! Are you kidding me? You need to cut the crap

and get this straight. Call him what he was—a pedophile who preyed on innocent young girls, leaving them forever scarred. You can be sure Joyce and I were not his first victims, and I doubt we were his last." Penelope felt her face flush, but she didn't look away.

"Calm down, Penelope. I knew this would upset you, which is the reason I wanted to meet in person. We need to talk about what to do going forward since it now appears he was murdered."

"Going forward? It sounds to me like it's going backward. You think because he was left-handed he couldn't fire a gun with his right hand. He must have figured out a way using another finger on his right hand to pull the trigger. The gun belonged to him, and his fingerprints were the only ones on the weapon," Penelope said, exasperated. "Elizabeth, I've made an effort to be understanding of your position in wanting more information about your grandfather's death. I realize learning what your grandfather did is disturbing, and I've tried to be considerate of your feelings. Now that you know what kind of man he was, what difference does it make whether he was murdered or committed suicide? His death was the best outcome for your family and for an unknown number of his future victims. You need to accept it and let it go."

"I can't let it go. Suicide doesn't make sense. If he planned to kill himself, why would he go to the trouble of using his right hand? Why didn't he leave a note? Someone took the law into their own hands. He was murdered. Regardless of what you may say about my grandfather, his life was taken. A crime was committed. There is no statute of limitation on murder. I will take the information to my supervisor to request an investigation be conducted. I realize this means you, your parents, and the Mueller family will be questioned."

"For the love of God, Elizabeth!" Penelope exclaimed. "Your grandfather and grandmother will both be dragged through the mud! Can't you let your family keep whatever pleasant memories they may have of your grandparents? Think how this will affect your children when it gets around school that their grandfather sexually molested young girls. Kids can be cruel."

"I have thought about it. I talked to my husband. I am an officer of the law. I know a crime has been committed, and it is my duty to seek justice for the deceased. It is what I have to do. We work on a number of cold cases that the public never hears about. My family will only know what I tell them. I can protect my children and grandmother."

As Penelope listened to Elizabeth, her arms folded against her chest, she could feel her blood pressure rising. When Elizabeth finished, Penelope leaned forward, put her arms on the table, and looked straight into Elizabeth's eyes. In a firm voice, she said, "Let me make this crystal clear for you, Elizabeth. You do what you have to do, but let me tell you what I have to do. I will make sure the media gets this story—every local and state newspaper and every radio and TV station. It may even go national. I'll do interviews and write articles. There'll be women who will come forward with their stories about your grandfather's molesting them when they were young girls. Granted, some may not be true, but it won't matter. I'll keep the story in the news till you have what you call 'justice' for your dead pedophile grandfather. If there was ever any shred of decency in your grandfather, it will be destroyed. Unfortunately, your grandmother will be collateral damage when it comes out that she knew all along he had been murdered. If you think you are going to put me and my family through this travesty and think your family won't be affected, you had better think again. You may be an investigator on the Dayton police force with connections, but don't underestimate me. I have my own set of strings I can pull."

With that, Penelope pulled two dollars out of her coat pocket, slapped it on the table for the Coke she hadn't drunk, and with head held high, stomped out the door before Elizabeth could compose herself to utter a word.

15

PENELOPE FELT HER knees turn to rubber as she quickly walked to her car. Her anger caused her hands to quiver as she dug in her purse for the car keys. The purse dropped to the ground, and her keys fell out. When she finally got in the car, she tried to steady her hand to get the key in the ignition. She wanted to get out of the parking lot before Elizabeth left the restaurant. Not bothering to put on her seat belt, she drove a short distance and pulled into the back parking area of a McDonald's. She needed to regroup. Confrontation was not Penelope's strong suit. She was a peacemaker, but when a situation was forced on her, she could hold her own.

She took a few minutes to collect herself, then dialed Reed's number. The second she heard the phone pick up, before he had the chance to say hello, she started talking. "Reed, this is Penelope. I hope I'm not bothering you. I've had an extremely disturbing meeting with Elizabeth. Do you have any time to get together?"

"Penelope, slow down. Take a breath. Why don't you come by my house? Let me give you the address. Charlie will be on the front porch to greet you with a two-paw hug."

"Wonderful, I need a hug. I'm not far from your

street. I'll be there in fifteen minutes. Reed," she paused, "thank you."

Charlie was on the porch announcing her arrival with two barks as he ran to greet her. Reed stood at the open door with welcoming arms outstretched. He was wearing black horn-rimmed glasses, and a strand of his dark hair hung casually on his forehead. He looked like Gregory Peck as Atticus Finch in *To Kill a Mockingbird.* She had to suppress the urge to run into his arms.

"Come in. You look a little frazzled. Take off your coat and have a seat by the fireplace. Let me get you something to drink—wine, soda, or something stronger?"

"A glass of wine would be great, white if you have it."

"White wine, it is."

Penelope began to relax even before she took the first sip of wine. Reed's house had an inviting charm. The fireplace was the focal point of the living room, flanked by two matching wingback chairs. Built-in bookcases on each side of the fireplace were filled with books, framed photographs, and a collection of small clocks. A sofa and coffee table sat along a wall that looked out the front picture window. Two smaller chairs and tables with lamps completed the furnishing. Artwork was uniquely displayed on the walls. The art was more contemporary than Penelope was accustomed to, but she liked it. There was no TV in the room.

Reed handed her a glass of wine and took the chair across from her at the fireplace. He had a beer in hand.

"Your home is charming. How long have you lived here?"

"I bought it ten years ago. It's a work in progress. It was built in 1960. The elderly couple who lived here had let it fall into disrepair. It needed major maintenance and updating. I had a small inheritance from my grandparents which allowed me to get needed repairs done. I'm pretty handy with a hammer, saw, and a bucket of paint and was able to do most of the inside work. My mother helped me with paint colors, fabric, and furniture placement. Some pieces belonged to my grandparents, which I had reupholstered—the chairs we are sitting on, for instance. I'll show you around the rest of the house later. First, tell me what happened today with Elizabeth."

Penelope began with the morning phone call from Elizabeth and then meeting her later in the day. She went through their conversation, trying not to leave out any details. She finished by recounting her final, threatening words to Elizabeth.

Heaving a sigh, Penelope said, "I think I may have stepped into quicksand."

"Quicksand? Do you think what you told her was a mistake?"

"I don't know if it was a mistake. I won't know until I see what her next move is. If she opens the case, I'll do what I said. I will not allow her to make Edward Werner the victim. Justice be damned; in my mind he got his justice. If he was murdered, he is lucky whoever killed him did it quickly. He could have been brutally murdered. I dread having to relive the repulsive event, and I dread it for my parents. In all these years, I have never told anyone—not my husband or a friend. My mother is the only one who knew, or so I thought. All my childhood I lived with the fear that if he found out I had told my mother, he would keep his promise and kill me. Of course, Mom told Dad and he went to the police. But I didn't know those facts until I read my mother's journal last week. Werner had known all along that I told. It gives me chills just thinking about it."

"It sounds like you left Elizabeth with some pretty threatening words," Reed said. "You said you had connections, strings you could pull. Do you?"

She looked at him with a gleam in her eye. "Oh no, I don't have strings. I have a heavy-duty, military-strength rappelling rope, someone with major media connections."

"Do tell."

"Do you know Augustus Marsh, or Augie as he is called?"

"Are you referring to the Channel 7 local evening news anchor and former newspaper reporter?"

"Indeed, I am. Augie and I go way back. He was a year ahead of me in high school. He was captain of the football team, class president, editor of the school paper, and damn good-looking—still is. All the girls were gaga over Augie and would do almost anything to get a date with him. All, that is, except for one girl—me. I thought he was a pompous jerk. Augie made it his mission to date me. Why, I don't know. I was a shy bookworm, not at all his type. Finally, I agreed to a date and discovered there was more to him than a good-looking jock. We dated, tried to be boyfriend and girlfriend, but it didn't take. I don't even remember if we ever kissed. What did take was a lasting friendship. We liked each other as friends and could talk about most anything. Augie went to Ohio State after graduation. I was at Miami University in Oxford, Ohio. One weekend, he invited me to Columbus for a football game and arranged for me to stay in the Delta Gamma sorority house. I arrived on Friday afternoon, but by that evening I was sick with a terrible stomach flu. I wasn't able to go to the game or the party afterward on Saturday. I fixed Augie up with a girlfriend—a great gal I thought he would like, and he did like her. He liked her so much they married three years later. I was the maid of honor at their wedding. Their firstborn, a boy, is named after me."

"They named their son Penelope?" Reed asked with a perplexed look.

"Sure, what's wrong with naming a boy Penelope?" She gave him a sheepish smile before going on. "No, Reed, they didn't name him Penelope. They named him Pennington and call him Pen. Pen is what my family and my good friends call me. He's now nineteen and a freshman at Ohio State. Pen is a fine young man. Plus, he thinks his Aunt Pen is pretty cool."

"I am learning all sorts of things about you today. I guess I should start to call you Pen. That's assuming I rate your classification of a good friend."

"I would say you are quickly rising to good friend status, considering how I dragged you into my predicament. Seriously, Reed, I can't begin to tell you how grateful I am for our new friendship."

"I feel the same way, Pen … Penelope. I think I will stick with Penelope for now. So what do you plan to do with this new information? When will you tell your parents about this latest development?"

"Not today. I had another bomb drop on me yesterday I need to handle. My husband wants a divorce. The papers arrived in the mail yesterday. I suppose I'm not surprised. We've been having problems for the past two years. I thought we would eventually work things out, but he obviously is ready to move on. His timing sucks, however."

"I'm sorry, Penelope. You haven't talked about your husband, and I didn't want to pry into your marriage. If you want to talk about it, I'm willing to listen."

"Reed, you have been more than giving of your time and ears for my 'intriguing situation,' as you refer to it. I don't want to burden you with another problem of mine."

"Being burdened is one of my favorite pastimes," he said with a smile. "Besides, I am working toward a higher friend classification. So, how long have you been married?"

Penelope had not discussed her failing marriage with anyone except the brief conversation she had with her dad earlier in the week. She glanced at Reed and shook her head. "I don't know how you do it, but here I go again— about to dump another load of my baggage on you."

She began, "We've been married twelve years. We met at the University of Colorado. He was finishing his law degree, and I was taking courses for my master's. After graduation from law school, he went with a medium-sized law firm in Denver. He opened his own practice eight years ago and is doing very well. Until a few months ago, I worked in his office. David is eight years older than I am. He was a product of the sixties—ponytail and all. We differed from the beginning. We had opposing views on politics, religion, and family. I wanted children, he didn't, but I didn't learn that till after we were married. They say opposites attract, but they don't always make good marriage partners. For the last two years, it seems everything I say or do annoys him. He moved to an apartment last month. I suspect he is involved with someone. He says he isn't, but his actions these last two years indicate otherwise."

"If you were such different people, what was the attraction?" Reed asked. "It sounds like you dated long enough to realize your differences."

Penelope gazed out the picture window, her mind drifting back to her life with David during their courtship and the early years of their marriage. David had a captivating personality; people were drawn to him. She was drawn to him. Being with David had opened up a whole new world for her, and she was thrilled when he asked her to marry him. Was it love? She thought so, and she had felt loved by him.

Penelope looked back at Reed and continued. "We dated off and on for three years—mostly on. I was a different person when I met David. I hadn't dated much and had never had a serious boyfriend. I was reserved. I didn't know how to relax or have fun. I took life too seriously. David was outgoing and spontaneous with an adventurist spirt. He uncovered my hidden sense of humor and taught me to be spontaneous, to be flexible, and to enjoy life. To put it simply, he captured my imagination. On the other hand, he is smart, a good lawyer, and a hard worker. We had a nice life for ten years, but he has changed, or I have. Either way the marriage isn't working."

"Divorce isn't easy, particularly when you have twelve years invested. "I was married for five years after I returned from Vietnam. The divorce was hard on both of us, as we genuinely cared about each other. For several reasons, we were not able to make it work. She remarried and has children, but we've remained friends. I've come to the conclusion that some marriages have a shelf life. It sounds like yours may have gone a couple of years past the expiration date."

"You may be right, but the timing couldn't be worse. "I don't want to tell my family divorce is on the horizon for me until this Werner business gets settled. I will wait to see what Elizabeth does. If she can open the case, I think she will let me know before my parents are contacted. The investigators will have to do research, go back through old police files to see if they have a case. It could take weeks or months. In the meantime, I am going to pay a visit to Mrs. Werner to encourage her to convince Elizabeth to drop her search for answers in her grandfather's death. She's in an assisted-living facility in Brookville. I just had a thought. How would you like to take a little trip with me to the enchanting town of Brookville, Ohio, one day this week?"

"I lived in Brookville my first thirteen years. I can give you the grand tour, which will take all of fifteen minutes max. I know a few former classmates who still live there. They own businesses and are raising their families in Brookville. Therefore, I would be delighted to accompany you, Mrs. Parker, to the enchanting town of Brookville. When does my lady prefer to make the journey?"

Penelope laughed, appreciating his effort to add levity to their conversation. "Kind sir, I appreciate your generous offer. I would prefer to make the journey the day after the next, if it meets with your approval."

"Madame, it does meet with my approval. We shall make plans forthwith for the journey."

Both were now laughing. Penelope needed the diversion. Reed had a way of soothing her nerves and making her laugh. She was looking forward to their trip to Brookville.

16

ON FRIDAY MORNING, Penelope and Reed were on the road to Brookville. It was a sunny November day. Most of the leaves were off the trees. There was a crispness in the air foretelling winter was fast approaching. While they drove, Penelope was pondering how to engage Mrs. Werner in conversation on the sensitive subject of her husband's death. She did not want to upset her. She needed to choose her words carefully.

Sensing her apprehension, Reed talked about his childhood days in Brookville, pointing out places of interest along the way. His commentary was sprinkled with humorous anecdotes. She was sure he embellished his stories to amuse her and to take her mind off her pending encounter. They drove by his grade school, the house where he had lived, his best buddy's house, and the park where the fifth-grade girl, slapped him for kissing her. Penelope pictured what Reed would have looked like at age eleven and found it hard to believe any girl would slap his sweet, innocent face.

Driving into the facility's parking lot, they agreed Reed would wait in the reception area while she visited

Mrs. Werner. The receptionist gave Penelope the room number, pointing her in the right direction.

Holding up crossed fingers, she turned to Reed. "Wish me luck."

Reed drew her to him, giving her a spontaneous, tender hug and a kiss on the cheek. She could feel her pounding heart beating against his chest. "You will do fine. Take your time. I have plenty of reading material."

It was a quarter to eleven when Penelope tapped lightly on room 110. She heard a faint "Come in."

"Mrs. Werner, hello. I don't know if you remember me. We lived on the same street in Dayton in the 1950s. Your granddaughter and I were friends."

"Yes, I remember you. You are Penelope Evans. You look much the same as you did when you were a child, except taller and no pigtails, of course."

"It's Penelope Parker, now. Mrs. Werner, it's nice to see you. I'd like to visit with you for a little while, if that's all right with you."

"Of course, it's always nice to have visitors. Please, have a seat."

"What a cheerful room. You have a wonderful view out your windows," Penelope commented, easing into a casual conversation.

"I spend a lot of time watching the birds, especially the hummingbirds. My daughter keeps the feeders full. I keep a record of the various birds with descriptions of each. I have named some of the regulars. The blue bird you see—he is Billy Bluebird. He hangs out with Bobbie Bluebird, a pretty female. When the weather is warmer, I open the windows. In the mornings I can hear the birds singing to one another as they flit from tree to tree."

Mrs. Werner's calming demeanor eased Penelope's nerves. She was a sweet lady who had the misfortune to marry an evil man. "I love the idea of naming your birds. I know they give you a lot of enjoyment. I've never been a bird watcher, but listening to you makes me want to learn more about them."

"They are fascinating creatures. I could tell you a lot about their habits, but I know you didn't come here to learn about birds. Tell me, what is the reason for this unexpected visit?"

"As you know, Elizabeth and I have been in touch. She is interested in learning more about your husband's death. I met with her two days ago. She informed me about her conversation with you. You told her you knew Mr. Werner had been murdered when you learned the gunshot was to the right side of his head. Your husband was left-handed and couldn't fire a gun with his right hand."

"Yes, that's true."

"This information convinced Elizabeth he was murdered, and she plans to get the case reopened. And that means my father, my mother, the Mueller family, and I will be interrogated. I tried to persuade her to let it go. Reopening the case will not only hurt my family, but also her family—especially you. I'm hoping you can persuade her to discontinue any further investigation. I realize this is a difficult subject for you to talk about, and I apologize."

"Penelope, I don't know what happened to you with my husband. I have my own guilt to deal with. I should have been more aware. I was young when we married. I was trusting. I never allowed myself to believe he was a bad person taking advantage of young girls. I suppose I should have known after … well, I can't … I can't explain."

"Mrs. Werner, please understand I'm not blaming you for anything that happened to me or others. My concern is I don't want this to get on the front pages of the newspapers, for the sake of my family and yours. You have more influence with Elizabeth than I do. I am here asking for your help."

"I told Elizabeth neither your father nor Mr. Mueller had

anything to do with Edward's death. I didn't want her to pursue an investigation. I thought she understood."

"Clearly, she didn't. I have to ask you: How can you be sure my dad or Mr. Mueller had nothing to do with your husband's death? Even I had my doubts about their involvement until I talked to my parents. I now am confident my dad was not involved, and I doubt John Mueller was. Do you know more about his death?"

Mildred Werner's calm manner began to change. She started a slow rocking movement. Staring down at her hands, in a whisper said, "Elizabeth will be the one to suffer."

Penelope leaned closer to her, placing a hand on her shoulder. "Mrs. Werner, do you know who killed your husband?'

Tears were rolling down the aged woman's cheeks as she looked into Penelope's eyes. "Elizabeth's mother."

"Oh, dear, your daughter killed her own father?" Penelope exclaimed, her hand flying to her mouth.

"No, no, not Donna! Donna is not Elizabeth's mother."

Penelope was now kneeling on the floor in front of Mrs. Werner. She put both her hands on Mrs. Werner's hands, attempting to console her while also trying to absorb what she had heard. "If Donna isn't Elizabeth's mother, who is?"

"Elizabeth will be devastated when she finds out who her biological parents are."

Trying not to upset her further, Penelope patted the woman's hand and, speaking in a soothing voice, asked, "Who are Elizabeth's mother and father?"

With tears in her eyes, Mrs. Werner said, "Nellie Jackson, our housekeeper, is her mother. Her father … her father is …"

A horrifying thought entered Penelope's mind. She hoped it wasn't true but feared it was. She reached her arms around the frail woman. "It's okay. It's okay. I understand. You don't need to say anymore. I think I now know who her father is. Her grandfather is her father—your husband."

Tears were streaming down her face as she gave an affirmative nod.

Penelope had a sickening feeling in the pit of her stomach. "Oh my, this will be catastrophic for Elizabeth." Her mind was a jumble of questions. Were Nellie and Edward Werner having an affair, or did he rape her?

Mrs. Werner gave a long exhale. She had stopped crying.

Penelope moved back to her chair. "Mrs. Werner, I don't want to upset you further, but why do you think Nellie killed him?"

"I need to start from the beginning. Nellie started cleaning for us when she was sixteen. She was a shy, respectful, young black girl. When she got pregnant, she claimed Edward had raped her and the baby was his. He denied it, but she swore Edward was the father. I didn't know who was telling the truth. I felt sorry for Nellie, knowing it would be difficult, if not impossible, for her to raise a child. Edward suggested Nellie live with Donna until the child was born. Donna didn't know Nellie was claiming Edward was the father. She assumed the father was a boy in Nellie's school. When Elizabeth was born in May 1949, she looked more white than black. Edward wanted the baby to have a good home. He convinced us that Elizabeth's life would be easier growing up white. That's when I realized Edward was the father. He arranged for Donna to be Elizabeth's adoptive mother. Nellie would continue living with Donna and help take care of the child. I don't know what they did about the birth certificate. I didn't ask any questions. I didn't like the idea, but when Elizabeth was born, we all loved her. Donna liked being called Mama. Nellie was able to live with her daughter and help raise and love her. It became our way of life."

Penelope's mind was overflowing with questions.

Trying not to register a shocked look, she asked, "What did Nellie's family think about the arrangement?"

"Nellie's mother died when she was twelve. Her father left her mother after her brother was born and has not been seen or heard from since. I don't think her parents were ever married. After her mother died, Nellie and her brother went to live with their maternal grandmother. It was all the grandmother could do to take care of her two young grandchildren. The thought of raising a baby was out of the question for the grandmother. The child would probably have been given up for adoption. When Edward offered Nellie the opportunity to live with Donna, her grandmother was relieved and very grateful."

"Is Nellie's grandmother still alive? What about her brother? Does he know Mr. Werner is Elizabeth's father?" Penelope asked.

"Her grandmother died years ago. Her brother, Jonah, is married with two children, and they live in Dayton. He is two years younger than Nellie, and she is very close to him and his family. Jonah was only fourteen when Elizabeth was born. He was an active teenager in high school, playing sports and, as with most young boys, didn't pay much attention to what was going on with his sister. I don't think he even knew she was pregnant. He assumed she dropped out of school to work full time for Donna. It was not uncommon in 1949 for teens to quit school for one reason or another."

"This had to be a big sacrifice for Donna. Having a child out of wedlock in 1949 was scandalous."

"In the beginning, I worried about Donna's reputation and was against the idea," Mrs. Warner confided. "She was twenty-five when Elizabeth was born. Her college friends were married and starting families, but Donna didn't have any prospects for a marriage. She felt adopting Elizabeth might be the only chance for her to have a child. Edward promoted that idea and used it to convince her to go along with the adoption plan. Donna has never regretted it.

"A few weeks after Elizabeth was born, Donna went to work for an accounting firm. They knew she had a child and was single but never questioned her about a husband. It was assumed she was divorced or widowed. It was so soon after World War II; some husbands came home a different person and marriages failed. People didn't talk about their personal lives in those days. As far as I know, Donna has never told anyone that she is not Elizabeth's biological mother."

"Does Donna know her father is Elizabeth's father? Is she aware he may not have committed suicide due to the location of the gunshot?"

"Donna doesn't know about the gunshot wound. She never saw the death certificate, and I never mentioned it to anyone until I told Elizabeth a few days ago. A year or so after Edward died, I told Donna Edward was Elizabeth's father. At first, she had a difficult time adjusting to what her father had done. Donna and Edward didn't have a close relationship, but she never thought he would do something so despicable. When she finally came to terms with the fact, she embraced the idea that she was related by blood to Elizabeth. For the first nine years of Elizabeth's life, Donna had been her surrogate mother. When she learned she was connected by blood, Donna's comment was, "No wonder I loved that little red wrinkled darling when she was born. I'm her big sister."

"It sounds like the arrangement was working. Why would Nellie want him dead, and what makes you think she killed him?"

"I don't know why she took such a drastic step. Something had to have happened between them. Nellie still cleaned for us, but Edward was never home when she was there. A week before he was found dead, I saw Nellie take Edward's gun from the bottom drawer of his

97

nightstand. She picked the gun up with a dust cloth and slipped it in her apron pocket. She didn't see me as I walked by the bedroom. Later in the day, I looked in the drawer to see if the gun was there—it wasn't. I never considered she would use it to kill him. I thought she needed it for her protection. Of course, I don't actually know whether Nellie was the one who pulled the trigger."

"I suppose not, but it's pretty incriminating evidence. This will be horrific news for Elizabeth. She has to be told soon, before she goes any further with opening the case." Penelope said, stressing the urgency to inform Elizabeth.

"I know she does. She should have been told years ago. Donna and I thought about it when she got married and especially when she was pregnant. Nellie is a light-skinned black, but we didn't know anything about her genetic background. We were concerned Elizabeth's children might have darker skin or other black features which would raise questions or cause a problem in her marriage. But they didn't. The boys have her dark hair, and their skin is even lighter than hers."

"I hope you'll call Donna soon to arrange a time to meet with Elizabeth. Once Elizabeth gets the ball rolling on reopening the case, she may not be able to stop it. Since it now appears Nellie may have been the one who killed him or knows who did, Elizabeth will have a difficult decision to make. I doubt she would want to send Nellie to prison for the rest of her life."

"I'll call Donna today. What do you plan to tell Elizabeth?" Mrs. Werner asked.

"Mrs. Werner, I appreciate your willingness to share this information with me. I know this has been a painful subject for you to talk about. As far as what I tell Elizabeth, I don't plan to contact her. If she calls me and wants to talk, fine, but I will not tell her I visited you or about our conversation. This is your family matter. She needs to get this news from her two mothers and grandmother. Come to think of it, you are not blood related to Elizabeth. But I know you love her like a granddaughter, and she loves you. You're the only grandmother she has ever known."

"Thank you for understanding. I'm glad you made the trip to visit me. To be honest, I have a great feeling of relief to finally talk about it. It has been a burden I have carried for far too many years. Although, I am worried how Elizabeth will react. Donna and Nellie will be loving and supportive, but this will be life-changing for Elizabeth and her family."

"Elizabeth is a strong woman. It will take time, but she will work through it." Penelope wasn't sure how Elizabeth would handle it, but she wanted to give Mrs. Werner some reassurance.

"I hope so. We all will be there to help her." Tears were beginning to form again in her eyes.

Penelope gave Mrs. Werner a gentle hug. "I hope we can visit at a later date on more pleasant terms. I want to hear more about your birds, and I will try to have some bird stories of my own to share with you."

Penelope's head was spinning as she left the room. Mildred Werner's willingness to reveal all she knew about her husband's death and Elizabeth's parents astonished Penelope. It was as though once the woman got started talking, she couldn't stop.

Reed stood up as Penelope entered the reception area. "You okay?" he asked. "You look a little spooked."

Before she answered, she hugged him saying, "You will not believe this. I can't even begin to process what Mrs. Werner disclosed. It changes everything."

He held the front door for her as they walked out of the facility. "Let's go to K's, my favorite restaurant in Brookville for lunch, and when you are ready you can tell me all about it."

"I'm not hungry, but you no doubt are starved. I'll give you something to chew on before you start munching on a sandwich. Elizabeth's father is—are you ready for this?—Edward Werner, aka her grandfather."

"Holy crap! He had sex with his own daughter? What a rat bastard! Excuse the language," Reed exclaimed as they drove out of the facility parking area.

"Your language is mild compared to what I would use to describe him. He is a rat bastard and worse, but no, he didn't have sex with his daughter, Donna. He raped Nellie, the black girl who cleaned for the Werners and helped raise Elizabeth. She was sixteen. Nellie is Elizabeth's biological mother."

With that Reed almost ran off the road.

17

IT WAS AFTER four o'clock when Penelope arrived back at her parents' home. She found them sitting at the kitchen table having their afternoon cup of coffee. "I'm glad you're both here. There has been an unexpected turn of events in the Werner case. Let me change my clothes, and I'll join you with the details."

A few minutes later, Penelope pulled up a chair to the table. "You remember I had encouraged Elizabeth to talk to her grandmother about her grandfather's death, and she did. Mrs. Werner told Elizabeth that when she read the death certificate, she realized her husband had been murdered. The death certificate stated he died of a gunshot wound to the right side of the head. Edward was left-handed. He could not pull the trigger of a gun with his right hand. His right index finger was injured as a small child, and the finger did not bend."

Penelope went on, telling her parents about visiting Mildred Werner in Brookville. Her parents were as flabbergasted as she was when they learned the truth about Elizabeth's parents and Nellie's possible involvement in Werner's death. Yet it was as though a breath of fresh air swept over the room, allowing an unexpected release of tension.

"This revelation takes suspicion away from us, and for that I am grateful," her mom said. "Nevertheless, I can't help but feel sorry for Elizabeth. Edward Werner was more of an evil predator than we realized. It frightens me to think what he might have been capable of doing. Will Mrs. Werner tell Elizabeth she saw Nellie take the gun from the drawer?"

"Mrs. Werner plans to call Donna today to arrange a meeting with the four women—Donna, Nellie, Mildred and Elizabeth," Penelope explained. "The plan is to inform Elizabeth of her biological parents and how she was conceived. Nellie doesn't know Mildred saw her take the gun. When she comes forth with that information, it will implicate Nellie in the murder. Mildred wants to tell Nellie privately first to get her side of the story, but eventually, Elizabeth will have to know about Nellie and the gun."

Her dad was quick to state, "Taking the gun does not prove Nellie shot Werner. A family member or friend of Nellie's who knew Werner had raped her may have used the gun to kill him. Nellie may not have known the gun was missing until she looked for it after she learned how he died. The gun was in the house where Donna also lived. Mildred said Donna and her father were not close. Did he do something to Donna? She may have had a reason to want him dead. Suppose it was Donna who Mildred saw take the gun. Do you see where I am going with this?"

"Yes, Dad, I do see where you are going. But I think we are getting ahead of ourselves. We have to let the Werner family have time to work through this. For Elizabeth, learning her parentage and that she is biracial will take some time to sink in. It will affect her family, her entire life. Let's not overanalyze it tonight. I've had enough drama for one day. It's Friday. How about I pick up some fried chicken and we watch *Wheel of Fortune* and *Jeopardy*?"

———◆———

Later in the evening, Penelope went to her bedroom, where she read the divorce documents. David's terms were fair and generous. It was apparent he did not want to have a fight over a property settlement or the amount of alimony. His eagerness to end the marriage saddened her. She suspected he would be remarried within six months.

With the two-hour time difference, it would be six in the evening in Denver. David was probably still in the office. Using the house phone in her bedroom, Penelope dialed the number. He answered immediately.

"Hello, David. "Why the big hurry to divorce me? You couldn't wait till I was home next week to hand me the papers so we could discuss it like adults?"

"I thought it would give you time to review the document and allow you the opportunity to tell your parents in person rather than in a phone conversation when you were back in Denver."

"How considerate of you," Penelope said, sarcasm resonating in her voice. "I'm not sure when I will tell my family. My parents and I are dealing with another matter. The last thing I want to do is add another worry to their plate. I'd like to think there is another solution to our problems other than divorce. It seems we should at least try to make our marriage work and not throw away twelve years of our life together."

"We've tried for the last two years. You're not happy, and neither am I. It's time to move on. I don't want us to end up hating each other over a bitter divorce. I have tried to make the split fair for both of us. If there is something you want, tell me. We can work it out." David sounded like he was negotiating a business deal instead of ending a marriage, but maybe they were one and the same to him.

"What I want is the marriage we had for ten years before it changed two years ago." Penelope felt a lump in her throat tighten as she choked back tears. She wasn't going to cry while talking to him, although she couldn't deny there was finality in David's voice. For him the marriage was over. She could not remember the last time she and David had sex. They had had a healthy sex life until he changed and no longer was interested in an intimate relationship. In the beginning, she thought he might have a physical problem and was embarrassed to tell her. She even considered he may be going through a midlife crisis and it would eventually run its course. Then, she began to suspect he had a girlfriend. The smell of perfume on his clothes when he arrived home from a day of golfing or attending a late business meeting was her first clue. For a year or so, when she rode with him in his vintage sports car, the lap seat belt was too tight for her. She had to loosen it to fit her size-ten lap. She figured the mystery passenger must be a size four—the skinny bitch.

"Penelope, I loved you, and I still care about you. I want you to be happy, but we're not good together anymore. You will find someone to share the rest of your life with. I know you will."

"It sounds like you have already found someone. Who is she? No, I don't want to know. It doesn't matter. I will sign the papers. I may need to extend my stay in Dayton. I will let you know." She placed the phone in the cradle, buried her face in her hands, and let the tears flow. She cried for the impending loss of her twelve-year marriage. But the tears were not just for the end of her marriage, as it had been over for two years. They were also for thirty-six years of pent-up fear, repressed anger, and the stress of dealing with those emotions the past few weeks.

18

MEANWHILE ELIZABETH WAS dealing with her own kind of hell. Donna had called Elizabeth at work to invite her to dinner along with her grandmother. Elizabeth's first reaction was to decline. Fridays were family nights with pizza and board games with her husband and sons, and her mom knew that. Elizabeth was annoyed by the dinner invitation. But Donna had said it was important, and there was a sense of urgency in her voice. Elizabeth relented. She would be there by six.

When Elizabeth arrived, she was surprised to see Nellie sitting with her mom and grandmother around the kitchen table. Elizabeth greeted the three women with hugs before sitting down at the table. The somber look on the women's faces gave Elizabeth an uneasy feeling—a feeling she was about to get some unpleasant news. Her hands felt clammy, and there was a heavy sensation in the pit of her stomach.

Donna began the conversation. "We have something to tell you which we should have told you years ago. We're sorry we didn't." Tears were forming in the eyes of the three women as her mother continued. "We want to tell you about your parents—who your father was and your biological mother."

Elizabeth's eyes widened and darted to each of the women, wondering if she had heard right. "My biological mother? What do you mean?" she asked, looking at her mother, confused.

"I didn't give birth to you, but I loved you from the day you were born. We all did." A tear rolled down Donna's cheek.

"I get it. You adopted me, but why have you waited all these years to tell me? It wouldn't have made any difference. You're my mother. I loved you as a child and love you now."

"There is no easy way to tell you." Donna looked at Nellie and Mildred, searching for the right words.

Nellie moved her chair closer to Elizabeth and put her arm around her. "I gave birth to you. You are my daughter, and your father was the man you called your grandfather, Edward Werner."

Elizabeth's mouth fell open and then snapped shut. She glared at the three women, trying to reconcile what she'd heard and struggling for a response. "What? How? Oh my God!" The color drained from her face; she felt faint. Donna got her a glass of water while Nellie and Mildred tried to comfort her. Elizabeth's body was shaking. Her thoughts were all running together in a tangled web. She shook her head as though she was trying to wake up from a bad dream. "You need to tell me everything!"

Nellie told her how she was conceived and about Edward insisting Donna be her mother so she could be raised white. Nellie had been grateful to be allowed to live with Donna and help raise her. Donna offered additional details and reassured Elizabeth that even though she was conceived under abhorrent circumstances, she was wanted by all of them.

Elizabeth wasn't sure she believed she had been

wanted, but she knew the three of them loved her. Growing up without a father in her home made her different from all her friends, but she never felt unloved or unwanted.

"This impacts my life, my children's lives. Why have you waited till now to tell me?" Elizabeth asked, demanding answers.

Mildred had not uttered a word so far. Elizabeth thought how painful it must be for her to hear again the story about her rapist husband. Finally, Mildred spoke, "Elizabeth, dear, looking back, we know we should have told you. There were times after Edward died that we discussed when to tell you or if we should tell you. We almost did before you got married and again when you were pregnant. You had a good life, the job you wanted, a loving husband, and two fine sons. No matter when we told you, we knew it would be upsetting. We didn't want to rock the boat. It was selfish on our part. When you visited me last week inquiring about Edward's death and said you were considering reopening the case, I realized we could not wait any longer to tell you. You needed to know about your true parents so you would have all the facts before you proceeded with reopening the case. We planned to tell you on Sunday. Then this morning, Penelope visited me asking me to encourage you to reconsider opening the case. In the course of our conversation, the truth about your biological parents came out. No one has ever known except the three of us. But since Penelope ..."

"What?" Elizabeth interrupted. "Are you saying you told Penelope Parker the details of my parentage before you told me? Why? How did that happen?"

"Yes, dear, but it wasn't intentional. It came out as we were talking. I didn't mean to. I am very sorry."

A range of emotions were going wild in Elizabeth. She was angry that the three women in her life she trusted the most had kept such critical information from her all these years. She felt betrayed. She could understand why, in

1949, the decision had been made to raise her as white, but she should have been told when she was an adult and certainly before she married. The idea of Nellie being her mother didn't upset her as much as the sadness in learning Donna wasn't her mother. It left an ache in her heart as though her mother had died. Nothing, however, compared to the shock of learning her grandfather was her father. Her thoughts were running together, she was scrambling to connect them in some logical manner. What was she to do? How would she tell her husband and sons? What would they think?

Elizabeth got up from the kitchen table and walked into the living room shaking her head in disbelief. She dropped down in the middle of the sofa. The three women followed her. Her two mothers sat on either side of her.

"I can't believe this," she finally said. "My head is about to explode. I need to have some time to get my thoughts together. I think it's best I go home."

Elizabeth wanted to get out of the house before her emotions took over, and she wasn't sure which emotion it would be first—anger, sadness, revulsion or confusion. She didn't want them to see her fall apart, nor did she want to unleash the anger she felt. She needed to be alone.

"Let me drive you home. I don't think you should drive while you are upset and have so much on your mind. We can arrange to get your car to you tomorrow," Donna suggested.

"I can handle driving home. It'll give me some time to think."

"Please call me when you get home." Donna pleaded.

"I will," Elizabeth promised.

They all stood up, each one gave Elizabeth a hug and told her they loved her.

She drove five blocks, turned into a bank parking area, parked in the back, turned off the ignition, leaned her head on the steering wheel, and sobbed.

19

PENELOPE WAS GETTING out of the shower when her phone rang. Grabbing her robe, she answered the call.

"How dare you visit my grandmother and force her to tell you who my father was!" If ice could have formed on the phone, it would have.

"Stop right there," Penelope countered. "I had every right to visit her, but I was not there to discuss your paternity. As far as I was aware, your paternity has never been a factor in your grandfather's death. I didn't force your grandmother to tell me anything. She volunteered the information."

"Why would she do that? You questioned me about my father. It's reasonable to think you did the same with my grandmother. You may not have asked her directly, but she is an old lady whom you could easily manipulate to get the information you wanted."

"First of all, you told me your grandmother was frail in body but not in mind. 'Sharp as a tack,' I believe, were your exact words. She did not appear to me to be someone who could be coerced into saying something she didn't want to say. Second, I was there to see if she would try to get you to reconsider opening the case. I had no interest in finding out who your father was. I never considered there was a connection. During our conversation, she made a reference to your mother. I thought she was talking about Donna. That's when she blurted out that Donna was not your mother. She didn't realize what she had said until it was out of her mouth. I thought I'd misunderstood her. My reaction was to ask her what she meant. If Donna wasn't your mother, who was? Then the story unfolded about Nellie and her husband. Ask your grandmother; she will confirm what I'm telling you."

Penelope was careful to skirt around the significant detail of Nellie and the gun. Mildred Werner had never told Nellie or Donna about seeing Nellie take the gun. Penelope wanted to find out exactly what Elizabeth had been told. Elizabeth's initial anger had subsided, allowing an opportunity for Penelope to query her for more details.

"Elizabeth, I can't begin to know how you are feeling. How did you learn about your biological parents? If you don't want to talk about it, I understand. But, if you do, I'm willing to listen."

"Okay." Elizabeth sighed. "I do need to talk about it. I have drawn you into this situation, and other than my husband, you're the only person, I can confide in."

For some odd reason, Elizabeth began referring to her family members by their first names. Perhaps it was her way of trying to make sense of her new family relationships or to make it easy for Penelope to understand what mother she was referring to while she was speaking.

"I met with Mildred, Donna, and Nellie at Donna's house yesterday evening. I realized the minute I walked in the house I was going to get some bad news. I thought one of them had a terminal illness. Donna got right to the point, saying they were there to tell me who my biological parents were. The three of them were struggling to find the right words. Nellie finally said she gave birth to me and my father was Edward Werner. I nearly fainted."

Elizabeth paused and then went on. "Donna lived in a small three-bedroom house on Wabash Avenue. She was twenty-five years old and working as an accountant. Edward persuaded Donna to let Nellie move in with her until the baby was born. At the time, Donna didn't know Edward was the father. When I was born, my features and skin tone looked more like those of a white baby. So Edward decided it would be best for me to be raised white. He convinced them I would have more opportunities and a better life being white. He persuaded Donna to act as my biological mother. The plan was for Nellie to continue living with Donna. Nellie would take care of me, allowing Donna to work. Nellie would've had a difficult time raising a child on her own. She may have had to give me up for adoption, if a couple would even be willing to take a biracial child in 1949. At the time, it was the best solution for me and for Nellie. Edward knew of a doctor on Fifth Street who delivered babies of young unwed mothers, which were then given up for adoption. He took care of having the birth certificate changed to list Donna as the mother, leaving the father unknown."

"I have to give him credit for providing a home for you," Penelope said. "But I have to wonder, what did he expect from Nellie in exchange for this arrangement?"

"I asked Nellie the same question. Her response was that she was grateful to him for giving me a good home and letting her be a part of my life. It was all she wanted."

"That may be true, but it doesn't answer the question, does it?"

"No, I suppose not. I was too overwhelmed to think about asking more questions. I was devastated to learn who my real parents were and hurt and angry that the three women I love the most had kept this from me all my life. I felt like the wind had been knocked out of me; I was barely able to breathe. My pulse and heart were beating so fast my eyes blurred. Of all the scenarios I envisioned over the years as to who my father might be, never, ever did I consider it could be Edward Werner. And I never doubted Donna was my biological mother."

"I can't imagine how earth-shattering this is for you. It will take time for you to process it. Mildred, Donna, and Nellie are a significant part of your life. They love you. I hope the four of you can work through this and continue to be a family."

"For forty-four years Donna has been my mother; now she is my sister, albeit half-sister," Elizabeth said. "Mildred was my grandmother, and I'm not related to her at all. Most unbelievable is Nellie is my mother and my grandfather is my father. It's mindboggling. This will have an enormous impact on my life. I'm biracial; my children are biracial. I know very little about my biological maternal family. I feel like I'm living in an alternate universe. I don't know who I am or where I belong."

"I'm sympathetic for what you are going to be dealing with. I'm glad you are able to confide in your husband, and I know those three special women in your life will help you any way they can."

"I will be taking next week off from work. I plan to meet individually with each of them. I have many unanswered questions. I'll be in touch." There was a crack in Elizabeth's voice, and the phone line went dead.

20

FIVE DAYS LATER, Elizabeth contacted Penelope. "I have had intense conversations with Mildred, Donna, and Nellie," she said. "I would like to meet with you as soon as possible."

"Would you be able to come to my parents' home tomorrow?" Penelope asked. "I have updated them on the latest developments, at least the ones I am aware of. Since we are all involved in this most unusual situation, I would like for my parents to hear what you have to say. I can promise you they will not be confrontational."

Elizabeth agreed. It was arranged for two o'clock the next afternoon.

Dottie Evans was nervous as the appointed time grew near. She had baked cookies and prepared coffee to offer their guest. Dottie was flitting around the den, fluffing pillows and straightening crooked pictures, when Penelope entered the room. "Mom, calm down. It's not Queen Elizabeth who is coming today."

"I know. I just want to make her feel comfortable when she's here."

"She will be comfortable if we are relaxed and you are not buzzing around like a bee in search of nectar," Penelope joked.

The doorbell rang. Her mom flinched and scampered out of the room. Penelope greeted Elizabeth and led her to the den, where her parents were waiting.

Dottie and Walt welcomed Elizabeth with smiles and a handshake.

"Let's sit at the kitchen table," Penelope suggested. "Mom has a fresh pot of coffee brewing, and I think I smell her famous chocolate chip cookies."

The kitchen table was positioned to look out a three-paned bay window onto a beautifully landscaped yard. A few beds of mums still had blooms. Squirrels were scurrying, foraging for the last few acorns to secure their winter supply. Two rabbits sprinted across the yard. The view was serene and peaceful.

"Your backyard looks like something out of *Better Homes and Gardens*. It's beautiful," Elizabeth commented.

Dottie poured coffee and set a plate of cookies on the table. "Thank you. We both enjoyed yard work for many years. Since we are older, we have hired an excellent gardener who does most of the work. We have promoted ourselves to supervisory gardeners. The yard still gives us a lot of enjoyment, whether we're sitting on the deck or here at the kitchen table."

Elizabeth started the conversation. "I appreciate your meeting with me today. I won't waste your time, so I'll get right to the point. I have confirmed that Nellie Jackson killed Edward Werner. After my grandmother, or should I say former grandmother, told me she saw Nellie take the gun, I went to Nellie's home to hear her side of the story. She confessed and volunteered to go to the police station, but I wanted to get all the facts before any decision was made." She paused. "For several years after my birth, Edward Werner did not attempt to assault her. Then early in 1957, he began coming to our house when Donna was at work and I was in school. He was there for one purpose: to force Nellie to have sex with him. The first time he tried, she was able to dissuade him by pretending to be sick. The next time she saw him pull in the driveway, she locked herself in the bathroom. He had a key to the house and let himself in. He pounded on the bathroom door, trying to coax her to come out by saying he was there for a friendly visit and a cup of coffee. Nellie stayed in the bathroom, refusing to open the door. She threatened to tell Donna what he was doing, but he snickered and told her, 'Donna won't take the word of a black whore over her own father.' Keep in mind, at the time, Donna didn't know Edward had raped Nellie and that he was my father. Edward said he would put her out on the street and not allow her to see me. To reinforce Nellie's fear, he threatened to kill her if she told anyone. 'Then, I will have Elizabeth all to myself,' he told her with a sinister laugh. With that, Nellie opened the door."

Dottie and Penelope both gasped. Walt murmured "Bastard" under his breath.

"You have to remember this was the 1950s," Elizabeth continued. "Life was difficult for black women. Edward was confident Nellie would do anything to protect me. I don't know how many times she was forced to give in to him. She didn't say, and I didn't ask. I didn't want to know." Elizabeth's lower lip quivered, and her voice cracked as she spoke.

"Let's take a break," Walt recommended.

"I'll get you some water, Elizabeth," Dottie offered, going to the cupboard for a glass.

"If this is too difficult for you, please understand you do not need to go on," Penelope said, putting a hand on Elizabeth's arm.

"Repeating the story makes it become more real to

me, if that makes sense." Taking a deep breath, Elizabeth continued. "Edward continued to taunt Nellie with remarks about me—evil, sickening, sexual comments. Since he had a key to the house, Nellie could not keep him out. At one point, Nellie told Donna she lost her billfold with her house key in it. She asked Donna to have the locks changed for fear someone would find the billfold and use the key to break in. Edward was furious when he discovered his key didn't work. But it didn't deter him. He soon got a new key from Donna. It was then Nellie realized the only way to stop him was for him to die. She began to devise a plan to kill him and to make it look like suicide. She took his gun from the nightstand when she was cleaning their house."

Elizabeth paused and drank some water before she resumed the story. "Nellie read the *Farmer's Almanac* almost as often as she read the Bible. The almanac predicted heavy rain and thunderstorms the week of September 13. The newspaper also stated there was a 90 percent chance of rain on September 13. On September 12, Nellie called Edward at his office, asking him to drive her to her grandmother's house the next day. She told him her grandmother was seriously ill and she needed to take some things to her. She said her brother would pick her up when he got off work at three that afternoon. The house was on a road off State Route 48. Nellie was familiar with the area. She and her brother had lived with their grandmother in a house at the end of the road. When her brother married, her grandmother moved to Xenia to live with her sister and the house had been abandoned. As far as Nellie knew, no one lived on the road. The property was only used during deer and turkey hunting season, which was over a month away.

Edward picked her up the next morning before he went to work. The weather was cool and cloudy, but it had not started to rain. She wore an old house dress, a raincoat, and gloves, and carried a purse and a tote bag. The road was a winding mix of dirt and gravel, dense with trees and heavy underbrush. Once you were fifty yards in, a car wasn't visible from the main road. Less than a quarter of a mile was a short clearing wide enough for a car to turn around. Nellie asked him to stop. The house was around the next bend. She told him she would walk the rest of the way. Nellie moved close to the door, opened it part way, pulled the gun out of her tote bag, and shot him in the head. He slumped over the steering wheel. She dropped the gun onto the floor where his right hand was dangling.

Nellie had a pair of men's shoes in her tote that she'd bought at a neighborhood sidewalk sale. Before she got out of the car, she put them. Also in her tote was the end of a garden hoe. She walked backward, using the hoe to erase her footprints, and got to the main road. She took off the men's shoes, put her own shoes back on, and walked a mile to a bus stop. There was a gas station at the bus stop where she got off. They had a large trash receptacle in back where she threw the shoes and hoe. As predicted, a downpour started two hours later. The rain took care of any distinguishable human tracks and other possible evidence. When she returned home, she washed all of her clothes, including the raincoat and gloves. Then, what she had done hit her, and she started crying and shaking uncontrollably. She has been praying for forgiveness every day since."

Elizabeth sucked in a breath, slowing letting the air out before she continued. "Nellie is the sweetest, kindest person I know. She shoos flies out of the house because she doesn't want to swat them to death. I can't begin to think of her as a premeditated, cold-blooded killer. I know she did it to protect me and to stop being violated by him. No matter how many times I have played this over in my mind, I still can't believe it. Learning about my biological parents has been devastating, but realizing I'm the daughter of a pedophile and a murderer is inconceivable.

It's like I'm in the center of a tornado with my life being twisted upside-down."

Walt, Dottie, and Penelope sat speechless, their brains searching for the right words. Penelope finally regained her composure. "Elizabeth, we don't know what to say or how to comfort you. We can't imagine how distressing and life-changing this is for you. The question is, what are you going to do now that you know the truth?"

"It's my major dilemma. I am an officer of the law. I have an obligation to report a crime. Nellie did say, if murder had been determined and someone was arrested, she would have gone to the police. She wouldn't have let an innocent person go to prison for what she had done, and she is willing to tell her story to the police. Nellie knows she broke the law and she should be punished, but she isn't sorry he is dead. It would be a stretch to have it ruled a justifiable homicide because her life was not in imminent danger. Regardless of her reasons, it was premeditated and in cold blood. I will have to weigh all the facts before I make a decision.

I'm aware of the impact on my decision. A hearing would be held to establish Edward Werner's predatory behavior. Penelope's testimony, Mrs. Evans's journal, and my parentage would become public knowledge. I know that would be unpleasant for all of us.

To help with my decision, I do have a request. I would like to read your entire journal, Mrs. Evans. I was only able to read a small portion of it when I first met with Penelope."

Dottie looked at Walt and then at Penelope, searching for their consent. Walt nodded, stating, "If my wife is agreeable, I think it is a fair request and would be helpful to you."

"It's fine with me. Would you like to read it while you are here? I can get it for you now. You can sit in the living room or at the table in the dining room," Dottie offered.

"Thank you. The dining room will be fine."

21

ELIZABETH WALKED INTO the kitchen, where she found Penelope reading at the table. Dottie and Walt were in the den, attempting to watch a football game on TV. All three had been struggling to keep their minds focused. Elizabeth sat down and slid the journal over to Penelope. "Your mother did a good job of recording the events and her feelings. I can understand your parents' anger and fear for your safety. However, I still would like to know what he did to you. The journal doesn't give any of those details."

"Why do you want to know those repugnant details?" Penelope asked.

"I think I have a right to know. Maybe because his blood runs through me. Maybe I want to watch for signs in my own sons. Maybe it will help me come to terms with the kind of man he really was."

Penelope picked up the journal and clutched it to her chest. She wasn't eager to share her experience. She recalled a phone conversation she had with Reed earlier in the day. He had asked her what she would do if Elizabeth wanted to know the details of her experience. She didn't have an answer for him. His comment was, "I think Elizabeth has a right to know." Reed's advice was always helpful, and she had to agree if Elizabeth wanted to know, she would tell her.

"All right, Elizabeth, I will tell you every detail. It may do me good to finally talk about it. I should have told my husband years ago. My mother was the only one I told, and it was never mentioned again. My family has a practice of blocking out unpleasant experiences. They figure if you don't talk about a problem, it will be forgotten and the memory will fade away."

Penelope's mouth was dry. Her hands were clammy. Perspiration was seeping down her sides. She filled a pitcher with ice water and placed it on the table with two glasses.

Taking a deep breath, she began, "I went to your grandparents' house Sunday afternoon to return a prize you won at my birthday party the day before. Your grandmother had left to take you back home. Mr. Werner had always been nice to me. I wasn't the least bit afraid of him. He said he was having a movie for the kids in the neighborhood in two days. He wanted me to help him decide which movie I thought the kids would like best. I felt special being asked to help. The movies were in the basement. I had been in their basement one other time, when it was raining and we played games there. I remember it was bright with cute pictures of puppies and kittens on the walls. There was a large chair with a table and lamp and probably some other furniture, but I don't recall. Sunlight was shining in the ground-level windows. It wasn't a scary place.

He started saying what a nice, sweet, well-behaved little girl I was. He asked me to sit on his lap and look at the movies together. I got on his lap. I didn't think anything about it. I sat on my dad's lap and on my grandfather's when we read stories. It didn't seem strange to me. He had three or four movies to choose from. We were talking about the movies, even laughing. I was wearing a summer pinafore dress that I had worn to Sunday school earlier in the day. Before I was aware of what was happening, his hand was in my underpants. I tried to get off his lap. I begged him to let me go. He pulled me back, holding me tight. He spoke in a soft voice, telling me to be still, he wouldn't hurt me, but it did hurt."

Penelope closed her eyes and flashed back to that day—the sight, the sound, the smell of Werner came rushing in, flooding her mind. A shiver ran through her body. She wondered if she could go on. She had to; she needed to tell her story. Too many years she had kept it a secret.

Elizabeth started to reach across the table. "You don't have to go on."

Penelope held up her hand. "No, I'm going to finish. I want you to know everything. Just give me a minute."

She continued. "I squirmed till I was able to get halfway off his lap, sitting on only one of his legs. I used both of my hands, trying to pull off the arm he had around my waist. He grabbed one of my hands and pulled my arm back. He held my hand on something that felt like skin and started moving my hand. My back was to him. I didn't look to see what he was doing. I was struggling with my other hand to pull the arm he had around me off so I could get away. By then, I was crying and begging for him to let me go. His grip loosened, and I was able to get off his lap. He still had hold of my arms. He turned me around facing him, pulled me toward him, and stuck his tongue in my mouth. Holding my arms, he looked me straight in the eye and said, 'If you ever tell anyone about this, I promise I will kill you.' It was the first and only time in my life I ever saw true evil in the eyes of a human being."

Elizabeth gasped. Penelope's heart felt like it was in her throat. They both reached for a glass of water.

"I ran home down the back alley. It was a typical

Sunday afternoon. When I had left, my mom was in the basement reading the Sunday paper. By the time I got home she was taking a nap on the basement sofa, and Dad was listening to a baseball game in his comfortable chair. He too had nodded off. My brother's bike was not by the back door, so I knew he wasn't home. I went in the kitchen, grabbed a bar of soap, and stuck it in my mouth over and over to get the taste and smell of that vile man out of my mouth. My hands felts sticky and dirty. I turned on the hot water, letting the water run on my hands till it began to scald me. In the bathroom upstairs, I took off all my clothes, threw them down the laundry chute, and took a bath, nearly rubbing raw every part of my body he had touched. The summer heat was still and stifling, but I was cold, freezing. I went to my bedroom, put on my winter pajamas, got in bed under the covers, and fell asleep. The next day I told my mother."

Elizabeth stammered. "I—I'm at a loss for words. I can only imagine the fear you felt and how this must have affected your life."

Penelope was trembling. She held her glass of water with both hands to keep it from spilling. "His words that he would kill me if I told anyone haunted me for the rest of my childhood. When you're eight years old and someone tells you they will kill you, you believe it. I never wanted to be alone in my home. I wouldn't walk outside at night by myself. I had nightmares. I became afraid of the dark and had to sleep with a light on. I still can't sleep in total darkness; I have to have night lights on. I keep battery operated lights in the event the electricity goes off in the middle of the night. As an adult, I realized Edward Werner was not going to kill me, but that childhood fear stayed with me. I dealt with other psychological problems. It may have helped if I had had some counseling years ago."

Elizabeth face was flushed, red blotches were visible on her neck. She looked like she was going to cry. The impact of what a wicked man her grandfather—her father—had been had finally become a reality to her.

"Penelope, I'm sorry for doubting you when we met three weeks ago. I didn't want to believe you. I didn't want to believe the man I knew and loved was capable of such horrific acts. What he did to you, to others, and to my dear, sweet Nellie— my mother—is appalling. I can't put into words my feelings and the sorrow I have for what you went through." Tears were trickling down both Elizabeth's and Penelope's checks.

Penelope reached across the table to Elizabeth with both of her hands, and Elizabeth's hands met hers. After a moment, Penelope spoke. "This has been difficult for both of us. The difference is, I've had thirty-six years to work through and accept my experience. You'll need time to process these life-altering changes. You'll need to grieve the loss of the person you thought you were and the loss of who you thought your family members were. But you have a supportive and loving family, which is a blessing, and that isn't going to change."

"Yes, I am blessed in many ways," Elizabeth agreed.

Penelope leaned back in her chair, her body began to relax. "As difficult as it is for you to learn what kind of man Edward Werner was, I hope it will aid you in making your decision on how to handle Nellie's confession."

Rubbing her forehead, Elizabeth said, "I will have to live with the decision I make for the rest of my life. No matter what I decide, it won't be the right decision. It will be wrong for me not to report the murder, and it will be wrong if telling what I know causes Nellie to go to prison when she was trying to protect me and stop him from abusing her.

Penelope, when we first met, you said I had brought this on myself, which is true. Then again, if I had not, I may never have learned who my biological parents are. As disturbing as it is, I'm grateful to finally know the truth.

Telling my sons and my husband's family is another hurdle. My husband will continue to be supportive, but his family may not. Having a biracial daughter-in-law and grandsons will not fit in their orderly WASP mindset."

"You're in a most unusual position. I don't envy you," Penelope said, standing up to indicate there was nothing more to say. Both were emotionally exhausted. "I hope you will let me know your decision. I'm extending my stay in Dayton till after Thanksgiving. You have my phone number." Penelope mentioned as she walked her to the door.

Penelope was drained after the emotional day with Elizabeth. She poured herself a glass of wine, joined her parents in the den, and plunked down on the sofa. "Whew, what a day!" she exclaimed.

"I would say so. How did you leave it with Elizabeth?" her mother asked.

"The reality of what a depraved man Edward Werner was has finally sunk in for Elizabeth. She has a great deal to think about, and it will take some time for her to sort it out. It's a lot of information to absorb, and all of it is life changing for everyone in her family. The future of her family depends on her decision. Elizabeth is a smart woman. I'm confident she will weigh the pros and cons as she analyzes all the facts before she makes any decision on Nellie's fate.

We parted on friendly terms. I let her know I would be here till after Thanksgiving and she could call me if she needed to talk. She is limited to the people she can confide in. It's not a topic you can talk to a friend about on the phone or over a drink after work. I'm glad she has her husband's support."

Penelope flung her arms out with gusto and said, "Anyway, I am ready to relax and enjoy the rest of my visit, starting now. Let's get Paul's family over here tonight for a rousing game of charades."

22

ACTIVITIES WITH FAMILY and friends occupied the following days for Penelope. She told her parents David had filed for divorce. They asked a few questions and offered their help if needed. Her mom encouraged her to consider moving back to Dayton. Actually, the idea had crossed her mind more than once. Before she returned to Denver, she decided to look at apartments in Dayton. She found a two-bedroom, two-bath, first-floor garden apartment three miles from her parents' home. At the time, she wasn't ready to commit on making the move back to Dayton, but the leasing agent agreed to hold it for thirty days with a two-hundred-dollar refundable deposit since Thanksgiving through Christmas was a slow rental period.

She sent David the signed divorce papers. He filed the petition for divorce the day he received them, and it was approved by the court on November 18. The divorce would be final in ninety-one days. Penelope made up her mind not to turn into a bitter, revenge seeking divorcée. David had hurt her, but she did not hate him. There were more good memories than bad in their marriage. David had to be given some credit for the person she had become. She liked that person. She would be able to navigate life solo.

The Saturday after Thanksgiving, Penelope returned to Denver. The divorce agreement gave her their condo, but she had no desire to keep it. She put the condo on the market, packed her belongings, sold or gave away numerous items, and marked the rest ready to go into storage until she decided where she would live. Colorado had been her home for the past twenty-three years, but her family and her roots were in Ohio. Her family tried not to pressure her, but it was obvious they hoped she would move back to Dayton.

In-between packing boxes, she called several friends in Dayton. Doug, Augie, and Reed were among those she discussed the merits of staying in Denver and those of moving. Doug and Augie didn't hide their delight at the prospect of her being back in their time zone. In fact, Augie went to great lengths to convince her that a move to Dayton was the right thing. He had his son call her, practically begging his Aunt Pen to move back to Dayton. Augie promised he would find her a job, and there was no doubt he could; Augie was the most Dayton connected person she knew. Doug was encouraging but not as persistent. He did jokingly tempt her with a promise of a lifetime supply of free doughnuts and coffee. And then there was Reed. When they talked, Reed was his usual upbeat self, always adding some humor to their conversations. On one such call, he told her, "I asked Charlie what he thought about your moving back to Dayton, and he gave a two-paws up." It was Reed's way of saying, he, too, wanted her in Dayton.

The day before the movers were to put her items in storage, she made her decision. She canceled the storage unit and made arrangements for a move to Dayton. She contacted the apartment leasing office and agreed to take a one-year lease. Her furniture would be delivered between Christmas and the first of the year. The week before Christmas, she loaded her 1992 Chrysler Fifth Avenue with as many boxes as it would hold and drove to Ohio. Her life in Denver was over; she was eager to embark on a new journey. A new year and a new life—she was ready.

23

---◆◆◆---

MOVING IN DECEMBER from cold, snowy Colorado to cold, snowy Ohio was not the best idea; not to mention the possible winter storms in states along the way. Reed had offered to fly to Denver and help her drive, but it would be a two-day trip, maybe three days, and that would involve other complications, which she wasn't ready for. Her dad and brother also offered to help her with the drive. She had kept a close eye on the weather report for the week, and it was good as far as ice and snow storms were concerned. Making the trip alone was what she wanted to do. She had stacks of music for the CD player and a variety of other travel essentials, including chips, chocolate, Pepsi, and water.

It was a welcome sight when Penelope pulled into her parents' driveway on December 21. The trip had taken two and a half days, but the weather had been good all the way. It was cold, but there was no ice or major snowstorms. Her mobile phone had been a good investment. Having the ability to call her folks when she stopped for the night or took a break from driving reassured her family. They had a phone-relay system set up that was put into action every time she called. Her mom or dad called Paul, who called Doug, who then called Augie. Penelope called Reed herself.

The Christmas holiday season was especially joyous for the Evans family. Her mom outdid herself with decorations and baked goods, while Paul and his wife, June, hosted the Christmas Eve festivities. It was organized chaos with June's sister and her family of five along with Paul and June's fifteen and twelve-year-old boys and five-year-old girl, Ellie, the "oops" baby who made the magic of Christmas come alive.

Penelope and Dottie provided the Christmas Day feast for the Evans clan. In the late afternoon, they all made a trip to see her apartment. The boxes from her car had been unloaded and were stacked in the apartment, awaiting the furniture arrival, now scheduled for December 28.

The day after Christmas, Penelope started spending the days at the apartment lining shelves, making a list of needed household supplies, unpacking boxes, and deciding on furniture placement. The movers arrived on schedule, and by noon they had come and gone, leaving her staring at a multitude of boxes and more furniture than she had space for. She needed help—she called Reed. No answer. She left a message.

Forty-five minutes later, there was a knock on her door. "Who is it?" she shouted from the kitchen.

"Welcome Wagon with housewarming gifts." Reed stood in the doorway, loaded down with two large grocery bags and a "Welcome Home" balloon tied to his wrist.

"You are the best gift, my knight-in-shining grocery sacks," Penelope said. Motioning for him to put down the sacks, she flung her arms around him. "I'm so happy to see you."

Holding her embrace, "I've missed you more than you know."

The rest of the day, they worked together, arranging furniture and unpacking boxes. Reed retrieved his toolbox from his truck so he could get her TV and desktop computer set up and hooked up her washer and dryer. The bookcase that needed to be assembled and the picture hanging would have to wait for another day. By six o'clock, her new home was livable. They collapsed on the sofa, Reed with a beer and she with a glass of wine, which were among the items he had brought.

"I would fix you dinner, but all I can offer is a turkey sandwich or a frozen pizza. I promise next week I'll prepare a meal fit for a king—or a knight, as the case may be." She vowed.

"I'll hold you to your promise. For tonight, how 'bout I pick up some Chinese takeout?"

"Sounds great. There's a place in the shopping strip down the street. I have their menu. We can call in our order."

Penelope had the table set when Reed returned with their dinner. They talked nonstop until Reed needed to leave to feed and walk Charlie. Walking to the door, he turned and asked, "Do you have plans for New Year's Eve?"

"Augie and his wife are having a party, and I need to make an appearance." She hesitated a minute and then asked, "How do you feel about going with me? We don't have to stay to ring in the New Year."

"You mean you're going to deprive me of the best part of New Year's Eve and make me miss kissing you?"

She blushed and blew him a kiss as she pushed him out the door. "Call me. I'll be here working away."

24

REED CALLED HER the next day, suggesting she take a break from unpacking and join him in seeing a movie. She appreciated his offer but had to decline as her parents were bringing her dinner. The next day, December 30, she decided she did need a break. She dialed Reed's number.

"Hey, there. Good to hear from you. What's up?" Reed asked, answering her call in his casual manner.

"I was wondering if your offer of a movie is still available."

"Yep, sure is. For you, there is no expiration on Remington offers. What would you like to see and when?"

"*The Pelican Brief* just opened, or anything you prefer is fine. What are your plans for this evening?"

"Tonight works for me."

They decided on the 7:15 showing of *The Pelican Brief* at a nearby mall. Penelope had a couple of errands to run, and said she would meet him at the theater. Reed was standing by his truck waiting for her when she pulled into the parking lot. It was a bitter, windy evening. People were dashing about with their heads down and collars turned up as they went to their cars or into the theater. Reed took

Penelope's arm, holding her close to protect her from the blustery wind.

"I have bad news," he said. "I arrived early to get our tickets. The 7:15 *Pelican Brief* showing only has a few seats left, and there aren't two seats together unless you want the front row, which I don't. They have held over *Indecent Proposal* with Robert Redford and Demi Moore, though. It starts at 7:25, and there are plenty of seats."

"Great. I wanted to see that movie when it first came out, but never got around to it."

Armed with a very buttery box of popcorn, they took their seats in the nearly empty theater. Only one couple was sitting at the far end of their row, and no one was directly in front of or behind them. They were enjoying talking and munching on the buttered popcorn.

"Do you know what the best part of eating buttered popcorn is?" she asked Reed.

"The mess it makes on your fingers is tasty to lick off?" he guessed.

"Nope, it's kissing with buttery lips." She looked up at Reed with exaggerated puckered lips. It took Reed less than a second to link her buttery lips with his.

"Hmm, you may be right, but I think your theory needs more testing." Reed reached in the bag for another buttery sample. He slid the pieces of popcorn in her mouth as she licked the salty butter taste off the tips of his fingers. Moving his hand from her lips, his fingers slightly brushed a nipple as his hand trailed down her side. A sensual tingling ran through her body. She moved closer to him, wishing there wasn't a chair arm between them. She took his hand and laced his fingers together with hers. He kissed her softly, his lips tracing the line of her jaw up her cheek till their lips met again. Heat was radiating from his touch.

"See what I mean about buttery popcorn?" she asked, looking into his eyes.

"I certainly do. I'll be your butter-lips anytime," he whispered and kissed her hand tenderly. "Your lips are delectable with or without butter."

"At least we got that awkward New Year's Eve first kiss out of the way," she said, leaning her head on his shoulder.

"By New Year's, we should have kissing perfected." He predicted.

"Oh, I think it's already perfected. For a guy who hasn't kissed a girl since he was in the fifth grade, you have managed to master the art," she murmured in his ear.

"I read a how-to book. It had pictures."

"Hmm, did you learn anything else?"

"Maybe." He kissed her again.

"If we keep this up, somebody is going to shout for us to get a room," she cautioned.

"I have a room a few blocks away. May I make a proposal?"

"Depends. Are you suggesting a decent or an indecent proposal?" Penelope asked, giving him an alluring gaze.

"Lady's choice."

"In that case, I'll race you to the car, butter-lips."

They both jumped to their feet. He grabbed their coats, and she grabbed his hand.

EPILOGUE

THE REST OF THE STORY

ON JANUARY 15, 1994, Elizabeth resigned her position at the police department. The reason she gave was that she wanted to be a full-time mom, which was partly true. The real reason was she knew she could not be true to the Law Enforcement Oath of Honor, which states, "On my honor, I will never betray my badge, my integrity, my character or the public trust. I will always have the courage to hold myself and others accountable for our actions. I will always uphold the constitution, my community, and the agency I serve."

Elizabeth could not justify having Nellie tried for murder and risk her being sent to prison. The time to have charged Nellie with murder was in 1957. Mildred Werner had the responsibility when she read the death certificate and learned the gunshot was to the right side of her husband's head. She should have advised the police then that her husband was left-handed and could not have pulled the trigger with his right hand. If Mildred had wanted to implicate Nellie, she would have let the police know she saw Nellie take his gun. For whatever reason, Mildred wanted to let her husband's death remain a suicide. And

Elizabeth wanted the same; Edward Werner had gotten justice.

Elizabeth's sons embraced being biracial; they thought it was cool. The boys adored Nellie and were thrilled to call her Nana Nell. They wanted to meet her family and learn about their background. However, Elizabeth did not tell her sons or in-laws that Nellie had killed Edward Werner. There was no need to; the ruling of suicide stood. No one needed to know otherwise. The story the four women agreed on was that Edward Werner and Nellie Jackson were Elizabeth's biological parents. No details of the circumstances were given to the boys. If they asked when they got older, Elizabeth would tell them Edward had forced himself on Nellie. They could figure the rest out. She told her family Edward had arranged for Donna to serve as Elizabeth's mother so she could be raised white. The arrangement allowed Nellie to be Donna's live-in housekeeper and Elizabeth's nanny, so to speak. There was no mention of the other girls he molested. The story made Edward Werner sound like a halfway decent man. Perhaps it was better that way.

After the initial shock, her husband's parents took the news better than Elizabeth had expected. The Scott family had spent time with Nellie, Donna, and Mildred when celebrating holidays and other family occasions. The Scotts had accepted them as part of Elizabeth's family and saw no need to change their relationship. Elizabeth continued to call Donna "Mama" and Mildred "Grandma." In time, Nellie became "Mama Nell." Elizabeth was the glue that held the four women together. She had held them together in their fabricated family, and she kept them together in their true relationship. They were family, regardless of their individual titles.

Elizabeth and Penelope never renewed their childhood friendship. Elizabeth eventually went to work managing an assisted-living facility. Occasionally, Penelope and Elizabeth ran into each other and had a friendly chat about work and family. Their conversations would end with both agreeing they should get together for lunch or dinner with their husbands. Neither one ever initiated the call to arrange it.

———◆◆◆———

Mildred Werner lived four more years, to the age of ninety. Penelope visited her twice during those years. Their time was spent talking about birds, the weather, and family. Edward Werner was never mentioned.

———◆◆◆———

When Mildred died, Donna was the executor to her estate. Going through a box of photos and other memorabilia of her mother's, she came across her father's death certificate and read, "Gunshot to right side of head." She had to read it several times to believe what she read. Her father had not committed suicide. Her mother must have known he was murdered but had chosen not to notify the police. She wondered why. Did her mother know who had killed him? It was a question she would ponder but not pursue.

———◆◆◆———

Nellie never married, never had a boyfriend. She was a light-skinned, petite, pretty black woman who caught the eyes of both white and black men. The few dates she had gone on when she was in her thirties were awkward and uncomfortable for her. Edward Werner had taken away any hope for her to form a trusting and loving relationship with a man. Nellie was content to fill her life with work, church, her brother's family, and Elizabeth's family. She rarely missed a grandson's sporting event or school activity.

A proud moment in Nellie's life was graduating from high school at age forty-five. Her pregnancy had kept her from finishing high school and it had been her dream to get a high school diploma. The principal of the high school where she worked arranged for her to take the necessary classes to complete her degree. Each day after the lunch period, Nellie went to classes along with the other students. The students knew Nellie and enjoyed having her in their classes. She helped several of them with their homework assignments and studying for tests. On a sunny June day, Nellie marched with the rest of students across the stage to receive her diploma. Her family, Elizabeth's family, her coworkers, and the entire student body stood with cheers and applause when the principal awarded Nellie her diploma.

The days following their movie night, thoughts of Reed filled Penelope's mind. They talked every day and saw each other often. In February 1994, she went to work for Montgomery County Children Services in Dayton. In January, Reed began teaching history at a private high school. The next year, he started a creative writing class as an elective for interested students.

Reed and Penelope spent as much time as possible together. They had a lot to learn about each other. Reed had an expanded vocabulary and enjoyed slipping obscure words into their conversations. She caught on to his word game and became a word master in her own right. They played numerous intense Scrabble games. She taught him to play chess, and he taught her to use a hammer and a paintbrush. They laughed a lot. They had fallen in love. Their talks often lasted for hours. They shared their dreams, their fears, and their past experiences. He talked about Vietnam and his confused life when he returned home. She let him read her mother's journal and told him what Werner had done to her. She didn't need a therapist. She had Reed.

On a cold, dark night three months later, Penelope was sleeping peacefully in her apartment when she awoke in the middle of the night. She got up and went into the hall, to the bathroom, and into the living room, and one by one she turned off the nightlights as she walked through her apartment. For the first time in thirty-six years, she slept in total darkness. Her fear of the dark was gone.

Seventeen months later, on Saturday, April 15, 1995, Penelope and Reed married in a small ceremony in the chapel at their Methodist church with only family present. The ceremony was at 2:30. Reed had chosen the time. It was 2:30 in the afternoon when Penelope first walked into his life, and she had been lighting up his life ever since.

After the wedding, a reception for family and friends was held at Doug's Doughnuts. Doug pulled out all the stops. The tables had yellow lace tablecloths; the chairs were covered in white with yellow sashes tied in back. Flower arrangements of yellow roses and baby's breath were on each table—yellow roses were Penelope's favorite. Doug had the mahogany bar from his upstairs apartment moved downstairs. Two bartenders served guests a variety of beers and wines. The food was catered, but Doug made the wedding cake. A five-tier graduated cake stand held an assortment of beautifully decorated mini-doughnuts. On the top of the fifth tier was a large decorated Boston cream doughnut with white chocolate icing and yellow roses—Boston cream was Reed's favorite. The bride and groom figurines on the topper were holding hands with a Golden Retriever sitting between them.

Doug had arranged for a piano keyboard and singer. The couple's first dance was, of course, to the song "You Light up My Life." Walking hand in hand to the dance floor, Reed gave Penelope a twirl with his right hand before pulling her into his arms.

ACKNOWLEDGEMENTS

I WANT TO thank my beta readers: Janice Cruce, Lee Hinkle, Chris Livaudais, Kaye Moody, and Becky Rishe. I greatly appreciated their time and input. Thanks to editors, Heather Whitaker and Liz Jameson. I learned much from them. Also, the helpful staff at iUniverse Publishing Co. To the Writers' Group at the Osher Lifelong Learning Institute at Florida State University who for the past ten years have read and listen to my stories and offered useful suggestions and always supportive. Last, but not least, I thank the friends who continued to encourage me to finish the book.

ACKNOWLEDGEMENTS

AUTHOR'S NOTES

THE OCCURRENCE OF child sexual abuse is difficult to determine because it is often not reported. It has been estimated by some researchers that out of every 1,000 instances of abuse, only 310 are reported to the authorities. Of those, approximately 90 percent of victims knew their abusers. According to RAINN, the nation's largest anti-sexual violence organization, every nine minutes Child Protective Services substantiates, or finds evidence of, child sexual abuse. They state that one in nine girls and one in fifty-three boys under the age of eighteen experience sexual abuse or assault at the hands of an adult.

Sexual abuse of a minor is any sexual touching or activity. It also includes non-touching activities such as exhibition (exposure and/or masturbation), showing pornography, photographing a child for sexual gratification or for sale of photos, solicitation of a child for prostitution, voyeurism, and communicating in a sexual way by phone, internet, or face to face.

Printed in the United States
By Bookmasters